# The Judas

Books by E. Richard Johnson

THE JUDAS
THE GOD KEEPERS
CAGE FIVE IS GOING TO BREAK
THE INSIDE MAN
MONGO'S BACK IN TOWN
SILVER STREET

The Judas

E. Richard Johnson

Harper & Row, Publishers
New York and Evanston

A Joan Kahn–Harper Novel of Suspense

THE JUDAS. Copyright © 1971 by E. Richard Johnson. All rights reserved. Printed in the United States of America. No part of this book may be used or reproduced in any manner whatsoever without written permission except in the case of brief quotations embodied in critical articles and reviews. For information address Harper & Row, Publishers, Inc., 49 East 33rd Street, New York, N.Y. 10016. Published simultaneously in Canada by Fitzhenry & Whiteside Limited, Toronto.

FIRST EDITION

LIBRARY OF CONGRESS CATALOG CARD NUMBER: 74-135184

For Miss Joan Kahn, who has been both editor and friend through four years and five novels before *The Judas* returned to her desk

The Judas

one

I stood outside the gray walls under the white sun and tested the alien smells of fresh-cut hay, and car exhaust, and the million or so other odors that never creep through the smell of disinfectant and sweat on the other side of Jefferson's steel gates.

I decided that the world still stank the same way it had five years before, while I stood in the heat at the bus stop and waited for something to happen, without minding the heat and sweat that made my shorts ball up in my crotch.

It was July 17, and the month had begun hot. It had begun, as the summer had, with a white sun to bake the country, then steam it into mirage-like patterns of distorted heat waves after the sudden, cold prairie storms that came steadily enough to promise a fair crop of wheat to the world of fantasy outside. The sun and sudden storms had promised only a good crop of sweat inside the walls, which wore the heat like a hot blanket and edged the pressing routine with quick tempers and sleepless nights. No one thought much about outside smells with the summer stink of a cell block in his nose.

So we don't really mind the alien smells of outside or the heat as we stand at the bus stop in front of the prison. Most of us come out and feel something while we wait: bitterness, sadness, or maybe fear. It creeps into you and makes you begin to live again, because the world events are no longer a review of distant, detached plays, read from a newspaper, or heard in the pygmy voice of the cell radio.

At least the lucky ones begin to feel and live again. The ones who are not lucky, like me, wait and test the free air without really expecting much, and nothing happens.

And after a while we snug down our state-issued, stingy brims against the sun and realize that nothing is going to happen inside us, because nothing has changed except the time is gone and we're a little empty inside —which helped put the early gray in our hair and a distant look in our eyes. It is an exclusive fraternity of those for whom the cards are all turned and there is nothing to do but play the game out. When you realize that, you congratulate yourself on the fact that the veneer you wear has not been cracked behind the walls. It is a simple rule: if you can't feel, you can't be reached; and you can go on doing whatever it was that had brought you to Jeff City in the first place. What had put me behind the walls had been a mistake on my part, and not what I do for a living. My vocation, if proved in court, would not call for only five years behind the walls.

They call me Judas.

For a living, I kill people. And that vocation calls for a good many more years than five behind the walls—if you're lucky. A more fitting description of my trade is: I am an assassin for organized crime, which means I can't be hired to arrange an accident for your mother-in-law, or such. I'm a gun for the Mafiosi. Call it Mafia, La Cosa Nostra, the brotherhood, or anything you like; it is an organization that finds use for an internal assassin. In fact, with the twenty-four or so family groups within the organization, and with each one wanting a larger piece of the American crime pie, there is seldom a lack of work, and little internal peace. That explains in part the Judas tag I'm known by. It began so long ago that I no longer need to work hard at quashing the memory. It began with a gray-haired racket boss who made a series of mistakes. The cops couldn't touch him, the local guns for the organization couldn't touch him. Me? I touched him, and he used his last minute on earth to hang a name on me that the organization never forgot.

My real name is almost as offbeat as my trade name. When I was born I was tagged Jericho Jones. Kansas City is my home town. I'm an even six feet tall, with graying brown hair and smoke-colored eyes. I look like Mr. Average in a crowd. The five-years-of-shade complexion that I wore at the bus stop went along with my slightly rusty reputation and the empty feeling I had.

I stood at the bus stop and studied the rented car that pulled into the no-parking zone in front of me. My glance fell on the driver as I lighted a cigarette and waited.

The kid in the car was like all punks who figure that they are in the big time when some boss starts paying them two hundred a week to do muscle work and run errands for local problems. About the only time a hood can be picked out of a crowd is when he's new at the game. He's got the eager look then, and the flashy dress to match his exaggerated swagger. And nine times out of ten, he'll keep that big-time illusion until he gets a bullet in the face for payday; or else he gets enough lumps put on him to mellow out some. Like I said, one out of ten stays, if he is fortunate enough to make it, and find himself a less risky job with the family.

Watching the kid in the car polish his sunglasses elaborately while he pretended to be interested in everything around but me, I didn't think that he would make the grade. As he got out of the car and came over to help me watch the walls, I wondered absently who had known I was getting out and sent him down. It was a good question to consider, since after five years "the Judas" was long-dead history, and people tend to forget your talents with time. I wanted it like that, for the time being anyway.

The kid was tall, about six feet two inches, with a

medium build and a go-to-hell swagger as he came across the sidewalk. I watched his eyes, half hidden behind the sunglasses, and deadpanned it until the grin faded from his face. He had blond hair and a weak chin below his thin lips, and the collar of his jacket was turned up as though he might be expected to start snapping his chewing gum next.

"You're Jericho Jones?" he said. "The Judas?"

I didn't answer for a moment, then I said, "No. I'm a DA on vacation; and you're a refugee from reform school with a lot of nose trouble."

"Not quite," he said softly. "I've seen your pictures. A little pale now, but still the Judas."

"I'm a little older too, friend," I said. "And I've had about an assful of questions to answer inside those walls. I might even be goddamn good and tired of answering them."

His eyes flicked over me and settled on my face, which must have reminded him that I could take care of myself. Briefly he turned his head and stared at the walls and the guard towers, before he spat on the sidewalk, saying, "I know how it is, friend. I did two long ones myself, over at Joliet."

"What for?" I wanted to know. "Baby raping? Or hanging around street corners too much?"

His lips turned slowly white and he let his hand settle into the pocket of his suit jacket. "I got a message for you, Judas, from my boss, or I wouldn't be taking that kind of crap."

I grinned at him. "Don't let business stand in the way of anything you figure that your ass can back up." I watched his face twitch, while the hand in the coat pocket remained still. Then I asked, "So who's your boss?"

"I'm Leo Powell," he said, and let his face slide back into the blank grin. "I been down here for three days waiting for you to walk out of those gates." He paused for a moment. "Tony Candoli sent me down from Chicago when he knew you were getting out."

He said it as though he had just named God, and waited for me to be properly impressed.

"He could have saved himself a plane fare," I told him. "I've been away too long, and I've got a five-year thirst to catch up on. I want to get laid and drunk, and maybe eat a good steak first—if that's not asking too much, that is." I searched my cigarette package and found a smoke. "You can tell him to pass the word too. It's been a long time, and maybe I won't be taking any calls for a while; maybe I won't be taking any, period!"

Powell sighed and handed over an envelope he'd been carrying inside his jacket. "That's what the boss figured you'd say." He shrugged. "So he sent this."

I opened the envelope slowly, viewing the finger smudges around the flap, and studying Tony Candoli's penmanship on the envelope. Inside there were five one-hundred-dollar bills and a note that read: "Five more for a talk, Jericho."

I put the money away and shrugged, wondering why a talk with me was worth it. And why it had to be me, when there were enough piece men around.

"The boss is a pretty sick man, Jericho," Powell said, like it would help me decide.

I stared at him blankly. "Yeah," I said. "He's likely dying of that new sickness you people have around Chicago. A bad case of Vanatta, I think it's called; and people who get it usually don't recover. I understand that a lot of Candoli's boys have been getting it." I smiled. "It's a real rare sickness too; a man usually winds up in the river with it. You know, floating around with the turds."

He looked at me sourly. "The boss ain't worried about Vanatta," he said. "All he's got to do is say the word and I'll take care of that punk."

"Sure you will." I grinned. "Vanatta is old-school trained. He'd turn you over and spit on your ass before he blew your head off. Don't give me that everything-is-okay-in-Chicago business. I read the newspapers too, and what I read tells me that there is some family trouble around that town. Old family trouble, mister. Like between Sicilians and Neapolitans; and that's a bit of feuding that's been going on since the old-country days." I paused a moment and studied Powell. "So don't tell me that all it takes is you to end a three-year gang war in the windy city. As far as I can see, Chicago is a good town to stay out of, for a man who's looking for a drunk and some tail, and who might be mistaken for a new hired gun."

"You're getting old, Judas. And too careful."

"I was born old, mister," I said. "And I reached thirty-four because I was careful. You can tell your boss to send one of his lap dogs around when the drunk is over. That's an advantage of working free-lance: no boss, and I pick the jobs that I want. When the drunk is over, I'll know if I want to work at anything again." I rubbed my face with my hand, trying to blot out the memory of expensive young thugs like Powell, and I thought about the slim seven hundred bucks I had in my wallet. A thousand dollars for a talk would give me a nice warm bed and a bottle for quite a while.

"Why not let the boss pay for that first drunk?" Powell asked, and smiled thinly. "I can arrange for a doll to keep you company too."

I stared at him. "You run errands, do business on the street, and pimp. What else do you do for the outfit?"

"I follow orders," Powell said tightly. "How about it? I got two plane tickets out of Saint Joseph; we can be in Chicago this evening. You get a job if you like what the boss says, and a grand if you don't. You can't go wrong with that, can you?"

I didn't smile. I knew I could use the money, like Candoli had known I could when he sent Powell. "Yeah," I said finally. "You can go wrong with a deal like that. You can get yourself killed."

He wore a puzzled look on his face as we went back to the car. That was one of the problems with a young hood —he never considers it possible that he can die. I'd killed too many men not to have a few ghosts around to remind me how easy dying was, and I'd come close to doing it myself a few times. I thought about that as we drove toward the airport, and wondered exactly what Candoli wanted.

The flight to Chicago was boring. I divided my attention between remembering what I knew about Candoli and adjusting to the feel of a free world, while the expensive young thug told me war stories about Chicago, and how tough he was. People don't change much. I used to tell the same stories myself and think that I was impressing someone with them. I remembered that when I grew tired of hearing a rerun of myself from Powell, and then I told him to shut up while I sorted out the things I knew about Candoli.

If you read the newspapers, you know that Candoli was the reformed racket boss in Chicago who got so much honey-sweet publicity from the press for his acts of charity. If you listened to the grapevine, you'd know who Candoli still was. He was the man in Chicago who got a cut of every piece of crime profit that the top Mafiosi squeezed from the city. He was the Mafia Capo, or Boss, or family head. But whatever you called him, and no matter what he put into the poor box, he was the racket man who had Chicago where the hair was short and the pay was best. That's how it was; pimps didn't pimp, boosters didn't boost, bookies didn't book, and whores didn't whore, unless Capo Don Candoli gave his blessing to the project, and received his cut.

The grapevine also said that Candoli's grip on the city was slipping, and had been slipping for the past three years. And the slippage wasn't being caused by police pressure, or public opinion either. It was being caused by one Joe Vanatta, a member of the family who had ignored the Mafia traditions and even the Mafia name, referring to the organization by the newer name—La Cosa Nostra—whenever he was around the old Dons, until the friction between the old and new elements caused a split in the family and in profits. Candoli, it seemed, was suffering from internal "family" troubles. I thought that it could be a fatal type of suffering when I remembered that the prison bookies were giving odds of ten to one on Vanatta being the next racket boss in Chicago. It boiled down to organized crime, and gang rule. I had to admit after all that there seemed to be some good reasons for Candoli to want to see me. And he had known what would make me come to the talk even on my first day out of prison. There never was anything like money to make a man forget reasons for not doing something. I had lots of those reasons, like thinking I was short on nerve, and being tired of feeling empty. I knew that I wasn't too wild about getting an organization contract, especially because that put you on the list of available guns—a list that there were only two ways to get off: either you died, and were considered safe; or you went to prison, and were considered too hot to use. Evidently I wasn't considered too hot to use, so I concentrated on old memories while the plane found Chicago in a light rain and as a taxi took Powell and me across town to a new apartment building on Michigan Avenue.

By then I was tired of the newness I'd seen, because the old had simply grown shabbier, so surprise took a little while to soak in after we left the airport, and even the dead, sick look in Candoli's eyes didn't reach me when he waved me into the Danish modern suite and sent Powell away with a flick of his thin hand.

Once Candoli had been a heavy man, heavy and solid, with a big frame. That was once. Now he was limp, skin hanging on a knobby frame, like a wet sack over sticks.

His hair was gray, brushed straight back, and his sick-looking eyes were sunk in dark pockets above a hawkbill nose and high cheekbones. I realized that whatever was killing him was doing it slow, and he'd learned to accept it.

The smoking jacket he wore hung on him like a shroud, a hundred-dollar shroud that didn't make him look any better than my state-issued suit made me look. He waved me to a chair and mixed drinks without asking, while he studied me like he would a dog or any man he wanted to use and knew he had to buy.

"You've got a good reputation behind you, Judas," he said. "The Kansas City boys still think that you ran one hell of a winning streak before your bust."

I wondered if I knew any of the people who remembered me so fondly, and took the drink he offered while I told him that a thousand bucks was a lot of money to spend for talking about my past merits and mistakes.

"I spend what I think I have to," he said. "I usually get what I want."

"You bought a talk, Candoli. You could have seen me at Jeff City any visiting day for nothing. I don't know what in hell you want, but for that kind of money I'll talk to anyone."

His mouth pulled into a thin line. "Like they say—a hard independent bastard, huh? That why you never asked to get into a family position?"

"I work alone because I trust myself," I told him. "There's no one to depend on that way. Any mistakes I make, I like them to be my own. More history?"

"You made a mistake that cost you five years," he said,

and tested his drink. "A good boy like you could have made room for himself if he backed one man. You could have gone a long way with the right people."

"The mistake I made was in taking a partner as a favor to the right people," I said. "It proved that I should stay working alone. And where would I have gone by backing one boss? To the same place, Candoli. Even the elite, old-line Mafiosi have a habit of feeding their peons to the law or to the river when the heat's on. Isn't that the code, Candoli? One must hold the family above all?" I shook my head. "No, thanks, I'll take a contract when I work. How much time will Powell do to keep you out of the slammer—if he lives, that is?"

Candoli waved it off. "He gets paid to take chances. I want you on this job because you've proved you can be trusted, and you work alone. Everyone in Kansas City knows that."

"Maybe I'm not ready to carry a gun for you. Maybe I'm not going to carry one at all anymore. Right now I want to eat a decent meal, sleep with a woman, and get drunk. A man can miss those things, or wouldn't you know?"

"I don't want to find out either," Candoli said. "I just hear what the Kansas City people know."

"Used to know," I corrected. "I told you, there's a few things I'd like to do before I take any work. I'd even like to find out what's going on around the country."

"I haven't got the time," Candoli said. "I'm dying, Judas." He said it as if he'd known it for a long time and it didn't scare him so much anymore.

"We're all dying," I said. "People do it every day. Some

do it when they work for you—in gutters. Did you fly me up here so I could tell you where sympathy is? It's right between *shit* and *syphilis* in the dictionary."

"I don't need your sympathy, punk," he snapped. "I don't want to just buy a gun either. A gun I could get for the five hundred you have in your pocket. You've got two things that I want. You know Kansas City, and you have your reputation."

He paused and finished his drink and I watched his hand shake when he picked up my glass. He was trying hard to be the gentleman hood with too many years of being Don Candoli behind him. He couldn't resist falling into his family role. "For the five hundred you have in your pocket, I could take this before the committee and get it done."

I smiled at him. "I don't think so, Candoli," I said. "I think this is something you can't take to the family and get a vote, or you wouldn't have me here. You people don't like outsiders that much."

"All right, I'll tell you why I want you," he said. "First, I know you've been used and are safe." He paused to spit on the rug. "We got people in the family I wouldn't say that much for. And so far as people know, you're not involved. Chicago's been good to me; it's still good. Maybe with the hot bloods like Vanatta coming in, it isn't like the old days, but it's good enough to make me want to keep it in the family."

I watched him. "So the lion is dying, and the dogs are coming to fight over the bones. Pick the toughest dog and let him have it."

"I meant blood family, Judas," he snapped. "That's the

trouble with you free-lance bastards. You don't know what a blood tie is."

"It's easier that way. You just die wherever you happen to be, and the state puts you away. No division of the spoils, no arguments over who gets your watch. I won't have any trouble dying, Candoli."

He studied me for a long while before he went to the desk and returned with a photo. "I want my son to have what I've got," he said. "Can you understand that?"

"So what's the problem? He's next in line to be boss. Just give him the bone, and if he can't hold it against Vanatta"—I shrugged—"tough."

"I would give it to him," he said, handing over the photo. "That's what I need you for. Find Johnny Candoli for me, or find out if he's dead. Either way you get paid."

I stared at the photo and recognized the hungry look. I'd worn it myself for a long time. The showy, hard look of a young hood in the rackets. John Candoli looked like his father might have once. He had the cheekbones, nose, and dark hair, with a hint of cruelty in his eyes that didn't go with the masking grin. He looked as tough, and solid, as any racket man can when he's trying to.

"How old is the picture?" I asked.

"A year," he said. "Taken last summer, I think. But he hadn't changed any when he went down to Kansas City a few months ago."

"You've got people in Kansas City," I said. "You got to be out of your mind to think I can find him if they can't."

"You know the people down there."

I grunted. "Hire the FBI, or something. I can't pull him out of a hat any easier than your own people can."

Candoli wasn't used to dealing with men he couldn't pull strings on, and it showed in his face. "Your five hundred is almost used up, Candoli," I said, "and I haven't gotten the least bit interested yet. Say something that will make me forget about a steak." I grinned and picked up my hat.

"How about Joe Noto and Mike Perille?" he asked. "And there's a late addition to that list, a friend of yours by the name of Blacky Shaw." He handed me a small newspaper clipping.

I read it and sat down slowly. The men he'd named had been part of his racket control in Kansas City, with Iron Mike Perille as its boss until some of the free-lance local talent had started to take over a few months ago; now they were numbers in the morgue file, and something I wouldn't lose any sleep over. But Blacky Shaw wasn't part of any racket or takeover. He wasn't anything but a boyhood chum, tagged Sanitary Blacky, a burglar, which was the one thing he was good at. I wondered how he had got himself on a dead list in a power grab, and who had put him there. I settled back in the chair again and studied Candoli.

"Curious?"

"Curious where John Candoli and Sanitary Blacky fit in. The rest is your concern."

"Perille owed me money and took care of that end of the business. I sent John down there a few months ago to look things over just before Mike got it."

"And?"

Candoli shook his head. "He did pretty good for a few weeks; maybe he did too good. A guy named Bicek—he isn't connected to anyone, Vanatta or anyone else, but the next thing I know Mike's dead, Bicek's running things, and John has vanished." He paused a moment. "People just don't vanish like that."

"Like hell they don't," I said. "Where does Blacky fit in?"

"He was killed about the same time John vanished."

"And that makes Bicek boss down there now; a free lance with no connection to the family." I paused. "Blacky just happened to get it at the same time, huh?"

"His was the last body known to turn up," Candoli said. "It made me think you might be interested."

"Why don't you send Powell down to take care of Bicek? I can probably manage to take care of whoever killed Blacky. No cost to you then."

"Powell's an idiot," Candoli said. "And getting Bicek won't help me find out what happened to my son." He thought for a moment. "It won't find out, either, if Vanatta is really behind that down there." He shrugged. "There's a chance."

I lighted a cigarette and told him the way I saw it. "You sent your son down there to play with the big kids, Candoli. So what do you want from me? Find where he's at in the river or the shallow hole with lots of lime they put him in? Or maybe you'd like the name of the man who put him away. None of those things will help you die any easier. I've been in striped sunshine for five years. Maybe I could get lucky and find out who hit him if he's been hit. I'd be more interested in finding out who hit Blacky Shaw."

Candoli watched me with an odd expression on his

face. Blacky Shaw was his ace in the hole, and he knew it. I gave him credit for expecting the answer I'd given him.

"We'll do it this way, Judas," he said. "You'll look for Shaw's killer anyway; so I happen to think that his killing is tied in with the rest of that Bicek mess down there, and with the same man who John ran into—if he's dead. So why don't you do them both at once and get paid for it?"

I studied the glass I was holding. "How much is it worth? Blacky I intend to look into. Your son sounds like unhealthy work."

"They say your word is good," he said softly. "You name the price."

I felt good about Candoli's troubles suddenly. "Dying or not," I told him, "I don't mind putting a price on work for you. I might be able to take care of both our problems: but the price is ten big ones for you—half now, half when I deliver. I don't mind bleeding you a bit."

It was quiet in the room and I could see the hate mixed with the sickness in Candoli's eyes. I wondered how much of it was for me and how much was for Bicek in Kansas City. It didn't bother me; there was nothing that he could do that would bother me.

"When can I expect my answer?" he asked.

"When I find one for you. A month, two—who knows? I'm going back cold, and people change in five years."

He shook his head. "A month is all I can give you, Judas," he said. "The doctors— One month." He waited a moment. "What else do you need besides money?"

"Names of people he knew here. Some I can talk to."

"I can tell you what they can," he said. "I don't want Vanatta's people knowing about you."

"I don't either," I said. "But I've got a reason for going back and being curious. Sanitary Blacky was my friend. So any leak will come from this end. Besides, don't dream, Candoli; your son's barber probably knew who Johnny boy was sleeping with and such. Did you?"

He didn't answer. He got up and went to his desk, and began to write. I finished my drink while I waited, thinking about Blacky, and how it must be to get knocked off when there's no one around to even the score and for something that you would not touch with a long pole.

Candoli returned and handed me an address, saying, "Kapsalis manages my club up there now. Him or the bartender should know who John had around more than I would. I'll have half of your money in the morning."

I gave him the envelope Powell had delivered to me, and waited some more as he went to the wall safe and took out the other half of our thousand-dollar talk.

I had one more statement for Candoli before I left. "The price goes up, Candoli, if Blacky's killer and your son's are not the same one. I owe Blacky a favor; your son is business."

Powell was waiting in the hallway for me when I went out. "How sick is he, Judas?" he wanted to know.

"Ask him," I said, and grinned. "Ask him nice and treat him good. Who knows, he might even give you a break like he did his son."

I grinned at his blank expression, and left the building thinking that it had taken me five years to get back where I'd started.

two

It was nine o'clock in the evening before I left Candoli's apartment. There were a lot of things he hadn't told me. There always are on a kill contract; but I was more interested in a meal, booze, and a woman than I was in a detailed report on how bad the racket business was going.

He hadn't mentioned the gutter war he was having with Vanatta, except casually. Maybe he expected that in my business, even as rusty as I was, I'd try to keep clear of that while I tended to the job. And he was right there; all I wanted out of Chicago was some information —I wasn't being paid to make a Syndicate kill. Bicek was a free lance, or had been, and since he was a Kansas City local I knew a few not so nice things about him, and figured that he could wait to be worried about when I got to playing in his back yard. Frankly, after five years behind the walls, I couldn't get out of Chicago fast enough. A power grab was no place to be testing rusty reflexes, and the risk of having to do that was always there.

It was still raining when I left the building, a cold and clammy rain that painted the streets a lead gray and kept them empty of citizens, who most likely didn't know about the silent war going on to see who bled them of the racket dollar. I knew. It's one of the things that you don't forget in this business, because it always feels the same—the brush of static tension in the air like waiting for a slow fuse to burn.

Gray streets and misty lights did things to me I didn't like, and made me eager to leave Chicago, so I checked the address that Candoli had given me and found a room just off Maxwell Street before I headed over to the club with the thought that the things I wanted would be just as easy to get in Candoli's Tropics Club as anywhere, and I didn't need to go first class my first night of freedom. I smiled to myself as I entered the Tropics Club. It was anything but first class.

But you didn't expect a swank club to be owned by a racket boss; you expected him to own a lot of clubs maybe, and they were usually the kind that you could buy anything in if the price was right. Candoli's bar was no exception. It was down on West Jackson, and even after a five-year absence I didn't feel that I'd missed anything. The place was the sort of dive you find in most run-down neighborhoods. There were dim lights made dimmer by years of smoke and dirt, and a general yellowed look to everything, a sign that advertised great fun for a Fourth of July of three years ago. The mirror behind the bar was laced with cracks that would distort the image of anyone who might be interested in peering through its fly-spotted surface to see what he looked like. There was a door to the can in the back on the left, which couldn't be missed from the odor that drifted out each time it was opened, and another door on the right that was boldly lettered OFFICE.

Past the bamboo curtain that separated the bar from the tables there was a small stage, and the girl who was taking it off to the drumbeat of a tired-looking combo was enough to make up for all of the other shortages the club offered.

I stepped over the guy who was snoring loudly just inside the door and treated myself to the first sight of true gyrating female I'd seen in a long time. She was doing for a bunch of loud slobs a strip that most girls couldn't match over on the magnificent mile. I watched the action with a rapidly drying mouth, and decided that it had to be one of three things: I'd been locked up too long, Candoli demanded the best of work in his dives, or the girl just liked to make love to a piece of lace by music, because that's what it looked like she was doing.

The few stumblebums spilled over the tables who were still able to pant were doing it, and I added my own heavy breathing to the music before I reluctantly pushed the bamboo curtain aside and entered the bar part of the club. There wasn't any doubt that the Tropics was a drinking man's bar. At that time of the evening, and out of seven men present, there were only four of us on our feet, including the bartender, and the two men at the end of the bar were on their way to join the prone crowd.

The bartender was a small man with quick, darting eyes, and a red nose that could have meant he sampled as much booze as he served. His name was Sam, and for five dollars he was the talkative type. Sam had seen a lot of men come into Candoli's place, and he'd learned a long time ago which ones were safe to talk to. For the things I had on my mind he knew that I wouldn't be there without Candoli's blessing. He brought me an extra drink so he wouldn't be disturbed and tried to ignore the strip act going on out on the stage.

"How about it, Sam?" I asked. "What kind of a boss was John Candoli?"

"What kind are they all?" Sam said. "He had a deep mean streak in him; but he was like the rest—they all figure they're Marazano when they're young. John was one of those kind who didn't figure things were happening fast enough for him. He wanted a big chunk of the action—right now. But he was sort of crazy, 'cause he made like he didn't care most of the time. You never knew what to expect of him." Sam sighed and grinned. "What kind of a boss is Candoli's son supposed to be?"

I tasted my drink and smiled. "You tell me. I don't remember things like that. Was he good, or was he just standing in his father's shadow?"

Sam glanced at me and looked around before asking, "How well do you know Mr. Candoli anyway?"

"Well enough to call his son a punk, if that's what he was."

Sam leaned over the bar and grinned. "He was a tough little bastard, all right. He was tough, with new ideas; that's why I think Tony sent him down to Kansas City and that Perille deal—to pound some of the old tradition into him." Sam paused and shook his head. "These kids now days, they always want things to change." He glanced toward the stage and nodded. "That's another reason out there why Johnny boy got a trip to Kansas City, if you ask me."

I turned on the stool and watched the stripper finish her act and vanish off the small stage. "Who is she?"

Sam rolled his eyes and began to polish a glass on his dirty apron. "That," he said, "is Peggy Allen, the finest little piece of female to grace our fine establishment in a long time." He leered a moment. "And the past property of old man Candoli, which is why she's working the dives instead of one of his better clubs. Like I say, that was one thing that son John had some ideas about too, and got sent off to Perille for them." Sam shrugged. "The old man don't come near her now, but he makes sure that if she works, it's in a dive. She's doing some hustling now too. I guess that's what the old man wanted—to make her put it on the street for fooling with Johnny boy."

I thought about it for a long time, then asked, "Is Kapsalis in?" I stared toward the curtain where Peggy Allen had vanished and added, "How's the chances of seeing the stripper tonight?"

"Kapsalis is in, all right," Sam said. "And the stripper has got one more act to run through before she's off."

"I've got all night." I grinned and pushed my glass across the bar. "I think Kapsalis can wait until tomorrow though."

Sam refilled my glass and pushed it across the bar to me. "Drink slow." He winked. "You'll need all your pep for the stripper, if you don't spend the night talking." He picked up my change and moved off. "Between the two, I'd say you made the best choice. Kapsalis is lousy company at night anyway."

Kapsalis, I decided, would be lousy company at any time.

By eleven-thirty, when Peggy Allen had finished her last show, I was beginning to realize that I would also be lousy company tonight. I'd been doing too much time remembering things about Kansas City, and five years ago. The whiskey and thinking brought back memories of another hustler, who had done the domestic bit around an apartment we shared when I was in town. Judy Vann had been a small blonde then, and she turned tricks because she made more money at it than she could make by sitting behind a desk. She made more money because she was smart enough to charge the tricks a hundred bucks a night for what she gave me free. And we had an agreement. She knew what I was, and left it alone up until the end. And I knew what she was, and where she spent some of her nights. I left it alone too. I paid the rent and bought her what she wanted while I was around. For that, I expected her not to turn a trick with one of my friends. Like I said, she did that for the two years we lived together. I made the first of my mistakes with Judy when she started talking about me carrying a lunch bucket instead of a pistol. I had laughed at the idea.

Now I stared at my whiskey and figured, as I had a thousand times in prison, that laughing at it hadn't been smart.

It had not lasted long after that, and I came back to the apartment one day to find the kid I'd been giving on-the-job-training to in bed with her. I'd just found out some other good news about him too—he'd sold me out and set me up for the other team that was playing the rackets then—and what I did to him wasn't pretty. It wasn't worth five years either. I still woke up nights sweating, remembering how perfectly Judy had set that up. I wondered who she was setting up now, and ordered another whiskey.

Sam brought me two, along with the news that Peggy Allen was finished for the night and would be out shortly. I slipped him an extra five, shaking myself back to the present. Feeling sorry for yourself gets to be a habit when you practice at it as much as I had, I decided.

I watched the room as Peggy Allen came in from the back, stopping a moment to talk to Sam at the bar.

I had had a habit with women when I was on the streets before. The ones I knew were hustlers, street-walkers, and cat-house whores. I watched the ones I didn't know, and priced them. I knew what the traffic would pay. Peggy could pick up a fifty-buck trick with little trouble. At her age, which seemed to be around her late twenties, that was hard to do. The eighteen- and twenty-year-olds had fresh youth on their side. Peggy really had what it took to be in the over-a-hundred trade; it was a sensual, almost animal sleepiness that showed in everything she did, and looking at her, you knew that she would be worth whatever you had to pay for her. But in Chicago it took Candoli to put her in the right spot to make that sort of money. In the Tropics she had her act, and a look at that was enough to make a man start opening his wallet; but for me it was hard to be objective about a woman when the nearest I'd been to a woman lately had been a movie screen.

And Peggy was one of those women who knew what she had, and took advantage of it, naturally and without seeming to. She had black hair, loose during her act and swaying with the drumbeat. Now it was up in a bun. Her skin was smooth, and dark, and her walk was natural and easy in four-inch heels, which is hard for any woman to master. She looked a young twenty as she walked across the room, and the clues to her age were in her eyes and in the tight little lines at the corners of her mouth, if you could look at that much woman and still want to search for things like that.

I didn't stand up when she reached the table, but she noticed the extra glass across from me and slid into the chair there. "You don't look like a cop," she said, "and you don't look like the usual customer. That leaves just a few things."

I smiled at the thought. "So what notch do I get set into then?"

"That leaves the new man Candoli brought in, for one," she said, and laughed nervously. "Powell told Sam all about the ungrateful bastard he'd spent the day with. I wasn't supposed to hear." She tasted her drink, and made a face. "You must be the ungrateful Jones."

"It sounds like this Powell is an expert at putting other people's business on the street," I said. "He must have leakage of the mouth or something."

"Anyway," she went on, "I like grim men who don't smile much, and seem able to give even Candoli a hard time if they set their mind to it." She glanced around at the bar. "And the kind who look at me like I don't have any clothes on."

I watched her over my glass. "I've already seen you with them off," I said, "so you don't need to sell me there. But just in case talkative Powell is wrong and I don't fit into any precut notch, would you settle for a guy who's going to take you out to dinner, where you can say all of the right things to him for a hundred bucks, and take care of the rest of your night's business too?"

"For a hundred bucks I'd probably tell you all about my sex life," she said. "What are we going to talk about anyway, Jones?"

"All sorts of things," I said, and meant it.

She shrugged casually, like she had an affair going with the loose bra she was wearing and didn't need. It was casually done, yet enough to make my hands begin to sweat as she looked at me levelly. "The hundred for a talk is nice. How's the wages for the rest of the night?"

"A business girl, huh?"

"It pays my rent."

I thought about the empty years and Candoli's money in my pocket, while I considered the reason she was working in a dive. I'd seen a thousand like her, the kids on the shady edge who get used, just like I'd use her. "How's another hundred?" I asked. "I liked what I saw on stage."

She nodded at me and signaled Sam for another drink, glancing around the bar as she did. "One more," she said, "and I'll take you up on that dinner." Then she stopped talking, and her eyes opened wide as her words trailed off. She turned her face away from the bar quickly.

I looked to see what had made that change, and picked out a new face at the bar. He was sober, not really out of place, but he had the look that said he was here on business, like I was, and not just to sample the rotgut. He was a heavy man, with a wide grin, and the object of his attention was our table. I bird-dogged him for a minute and watched the grin get bigger, before I turned to Peggy and was treated to a look of fear in her eyes keeping the tiredness there company.

"Who's your friend, kid? Does he think that this is a peep show?"

She shook her head. "He's nobody. One of Candoli's creeps, who thinks he's my watchdog. Candoli even watches the things he doesn't use any longer. He wants me to know how it is."

The creep at the bar kept grinning, and turned his head to spit some piece of wit at Sam, which brought a laugh and a guilty look toward our table. The creep with the grin seemed to be getting a charge out of my jailhouse look and Peggy's fear. He was wearing all the flashy trademarks of a new racket man, and kept enjoying the view of Peggy with a cold, flat stare that reminded me of two bugs on a fleshy rock. I pushed back my chair.

"Jones. Please!" Peggy said as I left the table.

"You look like you need glasses, buddy," I said when I reached the bar. "The floor show was over some time ago."

The creep didn't answer right away, just kept chewing the toothpick he had in his mouth as he casually slid his hand into his jacket pocket. He did it slow enough, and made all of the right moves so I wouldn't doubt that he had something in there besides his hand.

"Friend," I said, "I told you that the floor show was over."

He dragged his eyes over Peggy in a way that was obscene. "You did at that," he said softly. "But Peggy is all in the crowd, so no sweat."

"Tonight there's sweat," I said. "She's with me."

He smiled then, and looked at Sam over his shoulder, saying, "He's one day out, and already he's starting to lean. He might even be taking on more than what's his business."

I tossed a glance at Sam. "You talk a lot to everyone, don't you?" I switched my gaze back to the creep, and saw the grin slide away. "But I'll tell you what, friend. A man doesn't usually take on more than he figures he can handle, or what's his business, if his ass can't back it up."

"So he don't," the creep said, and let the grin crawl

back over his face as he turned to look at Peggy again.

He was faster than I'd expected when I grabbed his coat collar. His hand was already out of the pocket with a switchblade, as I spun him around and slammed his spine against the bar. He held the gut ripper like it was an old friend he knew how to use, but he'd forgotten that I'd just spent five years in a place where a shiv is like a toothbrush, and if I was rusty at anything, it was only in the gun department.

When he came away from the bar I kept him off balance, and got both hands on his knife arm. He didn't like it when the blade went past my stomach and up over the edge of the bar. He liked it even less when I brought the arm down on the bar's edge and the bones snapped like a wet pool cue.

He choked, and his face went white as he dropped the shiv. I kept him turning, his pain serving to cloud his judgment, until I had his good arm wedged up between his shoulders. He twisted some, but there's something about a man when he's off balance, and with his back to you, that will make him spread his legs and fight to get a steady stance. I let him spread, then went down low and brought my knee up into his crotch from behind, because the family jewels are just as unprotected from there as from the front. I heard him gag, and let him bend over, before I kicked him in the throat. I looked at Sam, who was standing very still with both hands on the bar.

"Your friend's a mess, Sam," I said. "You should have told him that I play dirty."

He wagged his head. "I just work here. He ain't my friend."

I reached out and picked up the switchblade, dropping it into my pocket. Then I knotted a fistful of Sam's shirt in my hand and held it tight, until his red nose began to purple. "Friend," I said, "don't be putting my business on the street. But seeing that you're so good at passing the word, pass a message on to Candoli for me." I paused. "Tell him I work as I damn well please, and if that isn't good enough, he can make other arrangements. I'll bury the next son-of-a-bitch that wants to play. Is that nice and clear?"

I let go of Sam's shirt and he nodded vigorously. Turning back to the table, I helped Peggy into her wrap. She was trembling under my hands, and only nodded when I said:

"Let's go get that dinner and a place to talk."

We caught a cab at the corner near the club, and I let Peggy pick the place for dinner. There didn't seem to be much room for questions as we drove across town. Chicago with rain, and sensing Peggy's fear beside me, kept me quiet. I rolled down the window of the cab, letting the city's stink in, while I listened to the traffic and tried to add up Candoli, and what had happened at the Tropics. It didn't figure. No one hires a man and then puts the dogs on him before he gets his suitcases unpacked. I smiled to myself. Candoli might want me dead, all right, but it would be after I'd been to Kansas City and finished the job. So the night's fun and frolic seemed to be a case of an overeager punk. I hoped that

Powell hadn't talked loud enough for Vanatta to hear the rumble. I was pretty sure he'd send more than a knife man to greet me when he decided who I was working for. I shook my head and sighed. Trouble always seemed to be one thing I could find lots of in a city, no matter how long I'd been away. But that figured; reality was never like the dreams I'd wasted hours on.

I slid my arm around Peggy, and remembered why it felt good to hold a woman, and I shrugged off the rest of the feelings.

I managed to relax with Peggy over dinner. After the fear had left her, she reminded me of Judy, and the thought must have shown in my face.

It was close to 2 A.M. when she looked at me over her brandy glass and said, "It's about time for questions, isn't it? Fun time is over."

I made a wet ring on the tablecloth with my glass. "You can tell me about John Candoli, Peg. But before you do, I know who and what Tony Candoli is. I take his money because racket money doesn't bother me, and it all spends. I'm getting paid to do a job, that's all. Before I start to do it, I want to know what John Candoli was like."

I watched the light fade out of her face while she remembered. It took her a long time, and the rest of the brandy, before she managed a tight little smile and said, "The truth is, Jones, that John Candoli was a cruel, crude bastard, who was very careful about showing it." She paused and chewed at her lip. "The sort of thing that he would have enjoyed would have been that animal staring at me in the club tonight. He would have enjoyed having him join us at the table, and then would have acted as though nothing was wrong."

I found a cigarette, and a light, and thought about it before I said, "Being a crude bastard is one of my talents too, maybe, but weren't you keeping in step with his father while you were playing musical beds with him?"

She ordered another brandy before she answered that one. "Keeping in step with Tony is a nice way to put it," she said. "Tony hired me, and I was shacking up with him at first. To put it bluntly, it was one of those things where 'screw the boss' was part of the contract. When I started working at the Tropics, Johnny thought that the contract included him too; he used that always available talent and charm he had to get what he wanted. He could be that way too, you know. He was only a bastard when he had everything where it couldn't be changed."

"What did he have to offer that the old man didn't?"

"A way out," she said. "He was young, and next in line for what his father had, as long as he kept him convinced that the old Mafia traditions were important to him." She shrugged. "And what does any guy promise a girl? It seemed like a way out of the clubs, and three acts a night."

"What did you mean by keeping his father convinced that he followed the Mafia code? Didn't he?"

She smiled. "John Candoli had his own code. He wanted power and position, and the old ways were too slow as far as he was concerned. It could be another reason that he was sent to Kansas City. His father didn't want a new 'Castellamarese war' here in Chicago if he could avoid it."

"He hasn't been doing any too hot of a job avoiding it," I said.

"Vanatta's like John was," she said. "Everything *now*, and a new family setup. They don't like to have to bring everything up before a committee meeting for the big boss to settle." She sat and stared at her glass for a moment, then added, "With Johnny gone, Vanatta has a good chance of changing things."

I grinned. "I never thought that I'd see the day—rebellion of the young in the brotherhood. That's almost as bad as an FBI man joining a draft picket line."

"It's not a joke," she said evenly.

"I guess not." I grinned, and worked at my drink. "But if John Candoli was what you say, why didn't his father wise up?"

She watched me silently for a moment, then: "He sent him to Kansas City, didn't he?" she asked simply.

"Yeah, and now he wants him looked for. Tell me about that business. What was the problem there?"

"What does it matter? People know that the old man is dying. Vanatta and Kapsalis are just waiting for that."

"He'll live long enough to pay my bill. I'm not picking sides in this, and I won't be around to fight over the bones. I come from a long line of cowards, Peg. It won't bother me to sit on the dead and enjoy my wages, but I won't be here to fight for a place in the daisy chain."

"You want it to be a joke, don't you? This is a fight for everything that's dirty in Chicago and Kansas City. The family control of everything. And you can't be near it without taking sides."

"I can," I said. "Because I don't care who comes out on top."

"The ones who can gain now—Vanatta and Kapsalis, after Johnny—they won't look at it like that. Why don't you leave it alone, and leave the dead in Kansas City?"

I watched her quietly. Myself, I didn't care if the job made Kapsalis worry about his position in the daisy chain, or made Vanatta worry about fighting a young racket boss instead of an old, dying one. I only cared about what they might do about me causing them to worry. It was a a point to consider, but I didn't plan on being in Chicago long enough to find out what they'd do.

I put my cigarette out. "All I'm interested in is history, Peg. About what sent Johnny boy traveling."

She thought for a moment, and said, "Why he was really sent, and what he said he thought he was going for, could be different. I was the one who brought him the message at the club. . . ."

"Tony wants to see you, Johnny," she told him. "He's sending you to Kansas City."

"Whatever you're taking, girl, quit," he said. "It makes you goofy as hell. I'm not going to Kansas City or anywhere else."

"I mean it," Peggy said. "Tony told Mike Perille that he was sending you down there."

"Iron Mike?"

"Yes, honey, Iron Mike."

"You know that crazy son-of-a-bitch thinks the Missouri River is the Siegfried line?"

"You could get away from this Vanatta mess, Johnny."

"Who wants to get away?" he asked. "Besides, I'm not going. I'm going to stay here and take you to bed."

"I don't think there would be room for all of us," Peggy said. "Why don't you want to go?"

"You know damn well why I don't want to go." He waited a moment, and continued. "That crazy dago will get me killed."

"Tony wouldn't send you then. He probably thinks it's safer there."

John Candoli grinned at her.

"You didn't have to tell him about us!" Peggy snapped.

"That's why he's sending me to the Siegfried line."

"For God's sake! It's just to get that mess down there straightened out."

Candoli smiled. "Dear old Dad is going to get my young ass shot because I've been screwing you. Everybody knows why you spend so much time down here."

"You never complained, you bastard," Peggy said. "I'd go with you if you asked."

Candoli seemed thoughtful for a moment. "Can't do it," he said finally. "I've got to see a man about making a million, and girls are a drag. I'll catch your act when I'm back in town. . . ."

She was silent for a long time break, until I asked, "And that was it? He just packed up and went?"

"That was it," she said. "He left and Tony put my strip act in the dive circuit." She held her glass up in a mock salute. "The end of a true romance, short and sweet."

"Yeah," I said. "True love is like lighting up when you

hear that Santa's coming; you always get turned off when you find out there isn't any Santa."

She looked away from me and watched the street through the window. The evening hadn't given me much except the news that a friend was dead, and a punk with a broken arm someplace in the city. And maybe the evening had put my name on Vanatta's list too.

It had been a busy day, I decided. I'd managed to get myself back into just about everything I'd left when I'd gone to prison, plus a promise of more trouble in Kansas City. I was beginning to believe that the Judas tag and trouble fitted me a lot better than I wanted them to.

I finished my drink and nodded to Peggy. "I guess that's it," I said. "Let's drop it. Tomorrow you can forget about John Candoli."

"Nobody forgets those people," she said. "They'll always be there."

I shook my head. "Not the dead ones." I grinned. "Forget it for now, and I'll get you home."

She gave the cabby her address, and wanted to talk about me on the way across town. "You don't like them," she said. "But you still work for them. Why?"

"The money's good," I said. "I make a living at taking advantage of their one weakness—greed. What the hell, do you like every guy you crawl in bed with? You do it for money."

Her mouth tightened. "It's easy for you to be cruel, isn't it?"

"It was a lousy crack," I admitted. "I'm not used to being with a woman."

I lighted her cigarette for her as she leaned toward me saying, "That's right. You've been away from something else for a long time too, haven't you?"

"You're looking at what's known as a five-year virgin," I said.

She smiled and moved against me. "That's one problem I think I won't have any problem solving for you. We've got the rest of the night for it."

three

The city woke me at six in the morning with the sounds of traffic outside Peggy's window; or it could have been five years of waking up to bells at that time that made me blink awake to the semidarkness and a moment of alien sensation, until yesterday came back into my mind.

   I rubbed a hand over my face, and felt Peggy stir, moving soft and warm against me as I reached for my cigarettes and got one started. There was a sour sickness in me from too much booze, and I decided that it was like a second act after a five-year smoke break.

In one day I was back to where I'd left the free world —with a contract on a man I didn't know, and with other men I didn't know eager to stop me from collecting. It didn't seem like any future to sell insurance on.

I made myself feel better by remembering that there was more to this contract than the money. There was Blacky Shaw on this one. A nothing burglar who'd spent the last thirteen years out of twenty in county jails, workhouses, or prisons, because there was a twist inside him that made him live up to the tag of Sanitary Blacky, so that he couldn't lick the urge that drove him to wash his hands within minutes after a job. He'd wash them in a mud puddle, with the cops chasing him, if he had to, but he'd wash them.

He was just another hood with a kink, but he was a friend, and he didn't give a damn what I was, so we could sit down and tilt a bottle while we remembered being kids.

I stared at the ceiling and wondered why I hadn't thought of Blacky in months, not until Candoli had handed me the inch of newspaper column about his death. It didn't seem like much for a lifetime summary. I felt empty with the booze sourness, and knew that if it hadn't been Blacky to use as an excuse, I would have found some other reason for taking the contract. He had only made it easier to do. And maybe he'd want his score evened with the rackets too. That was one thing Blacky always kept clear of. I couldn't see any reason for him to get four slugs in the stomach, in an alley, but I was going to find one. And if Candoli was figuring right, like he could be, anyone catching slugs in Kansas City had Bicek to thank for it.

I butted the cigarette, and noticed the wadded green of the hundred on Peggy's dresser. She had Candoli to thank for that, and she had been worth every bit of it.

I was grinning when I looked down and found her awake and watching me sleepily, her hair framing her face on the pillow. "Hello," she said.

"Almost good-bye time." I grinned, picking up my watch.

"You're leaving today?"

I nodded. "All I need is a visit to Kapsalis, and an airplane."

She put both hands on my shoulders and wriggled against me. "I couldn't interest you in another night, could I?" She began moving her hips, and her mouth touched mine, then pulled away. "A free night," she whispered.

I held her tightly, and saw the brightness in her eyes. "You're a working girl, remember?" I said. "No free ones."

She seemed ready to settle back on the bed, and then both of her arms went around my neck. "Okay," she whispered. "No free nights. But you get one for the road. . . . The night isn't over yet."

It was just past eight when I left her standing in the light from her door, and went down the steps to the city. I spent half an hour finding a bar that was open to help me over the taste of old booze in my mouth, and I went out shopping when I felt better. I treated myself to three good suits, and a small wardrobe with a dozen or so small things that a man never misses until he's down to the suit he's wearing and nothing else. By the time I was finished shopping I was back near the room I'd rented off Maxwell Street, and used that to change in, before I gave my state-made suit to a derelict and checked out of the hotel.

I called Candoli then, and found out that his disciple had made a mistake last night—a point that I could have assured him of, since I didn't have the broken arm—and then I found out where I could get a driver's license without waiting. He sent Powell over with the license, and the first half of my contract price. Five thousand in cash is an impressive sight. The way Candoli had gotten it, and my way of bleeding him for it, didn't bother me a bit.

I was still feeling pretty good when I caught a taxi over to the Tropics Club to see Kapsalis. A daylight view of the place was no improvement. It was still a drinking man's bar at eleven in the morning, only most of the customers were still on their feet, and Sam had put on a new stained apron to bring in the new day.

He seemed to be a little surprised to see me. His face, with its red beacon of a nose, turned gray, and he suddenly began wiping glasses off the bar instead of just the bar top. Then he looked about hopefully for a way out that he'd missed, and crossed his arms in front of him as he moved as close to the back bar as he could get.

I reached the bar, dropped a ten on the wet surface, and then gave him my best smile, which I'll admit is none too hot.

"Hi, Sam," I said. "Let's have a brandy with a peppermint floater to start the day off with, huh? Hell, give everyone a snort while you're at it."

Sweat was starting to creep down Sam's already damp face as he moved hurriedly behind the bar, opening bottles and pouring shots that half missed the glass. "What the hell's wrong, Sam? You got the early-morning shakes or something?"

"So help me, Mr. Jones," he said, "when that lousy Powell came in here yesterday, he never said a thing about—uh, about your work, so to speak; all he said was that Candoli had a new man, and his name was Jones."

Sam was shoving drinks in front of the other customers, and shivering as if he was working in a morgue. "That's why that dumb son-of-a-bitch was going to try you out last night. He was just going to scare you."

I knew Sam was lying, and the creep last night had damn well tried to put six inches of iron in my kidney. It's always nice to know that, for some reason or another, a member of your own team wants you dead. I could twist Sam a little and find out who had sent the knife last night, but that would only tell them that I knew all the rules of the game were not being followed. So I would wait and find out exactly who didn't like me for joining their side.

I had another smile for Sam when he brought me a second drink, and I asked, "Is Kapsalis in this morning?"

"Yeah. Sure he's in," Sam said. "Candoli called and said you'd be around, and that he had damn well better be in."

"Nice thoughtful boss." I grinned. "Or maybe he's just in a hurry for me to leave. How about me seeing Kapsalis?"

"What's your business with him?" Sam wanted to know. "He always likes for me to tell him what someone's business is, before they go back there."

"The business is my own," I said. "Tell him I'm collecting funds for the policemen's ball or something."

Sam shrugged, finished his drink, and picked up the phone. He talked for a moment then nodded toward the office door in the back and said, "Go ahead."

The office itself was small, but I could see behind it the apartment and card rooms which were used for gambling, and family business when needed. The apartment part of the office seemed to be the place where only a select few talked. It also seemed that I was not one of the select few. Kapsalis, in fact, hinted at that from behind the desk.

"All right, Jones," he said. "The boss said I should talk to you if you wanted a talk. Now what in hell is on your mind?"

Kapsalis was a man with a good thing, and he did not like the idea that I might disturb that. He was number one boy on the Candoli daisy chain, and enjoyed it. I have liked men less at our first meeting, but only when they were trying to kill me. Kapsalis was a little bit too much to run into all at once; he was too much like an overdone illustration of a hood. Maybe it was because he was pretty, and well oiled, and I do not like the gigolo type. Or maybe it was because he was trying too hard to be impressive with his three-hundred-buck suit, and I knew where he had to keep his nose to get the three hundred.

His feelings toward me seemed to be along the same lines, so I did not spend too much time with Kapsalis. I told him what I wanted to know, and he told me fifteen minutes of nothing before he said, "A dream. Old man Candoli has got a lousy dream about the return of old family tradition, because he's dying. He's up to his ass in trouble with Vanatta, and he dreams. I tell him to let me handle that." Kapsalis shrugged. "If there's heat for a while, so what? When it's over, we got us a solid bunch. I tell him to forget the kid, he's dead. But he's got to get you in to be sure. And the best part of it is that the poor fool don't know that John Candoli would forget old family tradition as soon as he took over anyway." He paused and watched me. "Like I'm telling you, the kid is dead. What do you want me to do? Find him for you?"

"Don't do me any favors, Kapsalis."

"So go look then."

"I will," I said. "But I wonder how they will fit."

He looked at me blankly. "How what will fit?"

"The shoes you're wearing to kiss Candoli's ass," I told him. "They belong to John Candoli, you know. And maybe the old man will change his mind about who's going to be wearing them when I find out what stinks about this mess."

He called me a son-of-a-bitch, and I thought that maybe I shouldn't have said what I said as I closed the office door and went back out through the bar.

It took me half an hour to reach the airport. As the ground vanished under the clouds, I used the time to

45

work on what might have been John Candoli's thoughts. Being of the new school, he would feel tough. Tough and eager to see the falling empire of Iron Mike, who was of the old school and trying desperately to hold what he had. I had one advantage on John Candoli. I knew what Iron Mike's empire had been.

From the dirty waters of the Kansas River by Ninth Street, over to the Paseo, with the Viaduct and Thirty-ninth Street to form its flanking borders, it was a garbage-littered, decaying empire, filled with the dregs of humanity and oozing the cruelties and perversions that people carry with them when they go there.

John Candoli would have like it, I decided. It was filled with the closed-mouth poor who stayed because there was nowhere else to go. And better yet, he would have liked the presence of the pimps, whores, derelicts, and jack rollers, of dope and death. And the thugs and thugs' disciples were there to make John Candoli feel right at home. He would have liked best the money the area would bleed when it was squeezed in the way he'd been taught to squeeze.

I used to like it. It had been my sanctuary when I needed a rest. Its dark alleys hid me from the hard-faced bulls who patrolled it, and it hadn't bothered me that Iron Mike had run it, because I didn't squeeze for any of the rackets. Nor had it bothered me who had run the smaller empire across the river, when it was easier and safer to hide over there.

I turned the old thoughts over in my mind, and it was like stirring moldy lumps in a damp cellar, because things had changed. I remembered now the city I'd been born in and knew that there would be nothing happy about my homecoming. I would find the same old thug's disciple jack-rolling a derelict for a dime, and a pimply-faced sixteen-year-old pimping for his fifteen-year-old sister.

It was the way my kind lived. We had always lived with only varying grades of status to separate us. We reached our grade, and were always that. A pimp at twelve was a pimp in memory when he drove a milk truck in the suburbs. A fifteen-year-old whore was still a whore in memory when she had a husband and four kids; at least to the ones who remembered her escape with envy.

I had escaped, and now I was returning, one of those they didn't name, and only whispered about. As I sat on the plane I could smell the stink of the river that the hot summer used to bring. And I knew what sort of stink there would be when I stirred up the waters to get the answers Candoli wanted. But I knew that I'd do the stirring anyway: there was Blacky, and Candoli's money, to make me do it. I'd taken contracts for lesser reasons. I was ready when I reached Kansas City, but I was not eager.

I caught a cab at the airport, and found a cheap apartment away from the river. For the next three days I left the apartment twice, to eat and to buy more booze. I was home, and I drank to that, until on the morning of the fourth day I woke up looking at a half-filled bottle and knew that the drunk was over.

It was only seven o'clock and the day promised to be cold, with hail and rain, as a Kansas summer day can be;

a crop-buster, the farmers call it— I was sick with the sour, shaking sickness that always followed cheap whiskey and little food. I gagged down a watered drink to help me shave, and poured the rest of the bottle into the sink. I showered and changed, smelling the sweat in my wrinkled clothes. It took a forced breakfast and extra coffee to send me looking for a cop.

There are several ways to dig up old news. A newspaper morgue would tell me the dates and places of people's death. But the cops would know where the live ones I was interested in were, and those would tell me a lot more about Blacky and John Candoli.

I suppose I went looking for Ferris because I knew he would be looking for me. He would want to say all the things a cop is supposed to say to a hood getting out of prison. And Nick Ferris did things by the book when it suited his purpose. He had been one of those cops who would stop and have a beer with a bunch of the locals, back when he was pounding a beat; but the local talent didn't let him catch them with a pistol or a sack of burglary tools. From what I'd heard, he was still that sort of a cop, but he was uptown now, in a detective's suit. And since he was in the homicide squad, he would know I was out, so I called and told him where I was. He told me where to meet him.

Detective Nick Ferris was about my age; but without the emptiness to help turn his hair gray early. His eyes smiled when his mouth did, but that was not often, and he was still a cop doing a job that he was tired of having to do.

"You look like hell, Jericho. You look like a lot of bad

nights," he said, as we sat down with coffee. "You didn't need to catch up on everything all at once, you know."

"I wish I could tell you the same thing," I said. "But the years didn't hurt you any, Ferris. How's being a cop these days?"

He sipped his coffee and studied me. "Being a cop is almost as bad as being a hood. I'm almost as unpopular in certain places as the Judas is. Only it seems that the Judas got a longer vacation than a cop does." He paused, rubbing his tired eyes. "I was hoping you wouldn't come back here, Jericho. Why do you people come back to the same holes?"

"It's home."

"Bullshit," he said. "Home for you has been where you unpack a suitcase for twenty-some years. But you had to come back here. So what did you bring with you, Jericho? You've been out a few days, and we have a squeal on you already."

I didn't wonder about the squeal. There is always the uncontrollable seepage of rumors around the rackets and anyone who touches them. I grinned at him. "You should have gotten all of my press clippings, Ferris. The stoolies would have buried you in rumors then."

He watched me impatiently, sipped his coffee, fired up a foul-smelling cigar, and repeated, "I said I had a squeal on you."

"I suppose that it's an airtight case too, huh? Maybe I pushed someone last night, and you've got fifty witnesses?"

He leaned over the table, giving me a smell of the cigar. His voice was thin and low, like it gets when he's mad. "Jericho. I have a police report on you, and I don't like it. I also have several bodies that have turned up this summer with holes in them. And I've got Bicek here —I don't need *you* around. I don't need any more dead men in town."

I picked up my coffee slowly and stared at him. "What's that supposed to mean?"

"You know what it means," he said. "If I can ever prove you're what the rumors say, I'll lock you up for life." He spoke flatly, just telling me how it was. "Now let's try it again. Why'd you come back here?"

"It's home."

Ferris shook his head and reached inside his coat, pulling some folded papers out. He slapped the back of his hand with them. "It's all down here. From the day you walked out of Jeff City, until you took the plane here from Chicago. And I've got a stack of stoolie papers besides. Nobody forgot you, Jericho."

I sighed, and wondered who the son-of-a-bitch was who'd passed on the word from Chicago. "They didn't have anything to remember," I said. "I went up for working over a cat who was shacking up with my girl. That's it. Read the record, Ferris. There's no other proof." I grinned at him.

"One of these days," he said evenly, "I'm going to get a night call to count the holes in you. But go ahead, play your games. Sooner or later you'll make a mistake. You, Bicek, or your two Chicago friends."

"Is that why you hate to see old home-town boys come back—you're getting imports?"

Ferris smashed his cigar out in the ashtray angrily.

"Sure," he said. "And just like you, they're trouble. A couple of hoods called Otto and Jo-Jo." He paused. "Probably friends of yours. Where in hell have you been for the past few days anyway?"

"I've been on a drunk—alone."

"Bull! Give yourself a break and take a look around. There's a lot of world out there to see. Use your head. All you can get in this city is trouble. I don't need you or out-of-town hoods around here."

"So you've told me. Tell this Otto and Jo-Jo to go home then," I said. "They've got nothing to do with me."

"That's nice," Ferris said. "Because the first man they started asking questions about when they got off the plane was you. They must be planning a surprise party for you or something. But when I add up those two, and Bicek's bunch, and you coming back, it makes me lose sleep nights."

"Can't your stoolies calm your nerves?"

"They know what they think; like maybe Bicek is up against a hard wall. Like maybe this gutter war didn't end at Perille, and I've got more trouble."

I grinned. "I didn't come back for trouble. I want to see some friends, and have a few drinks."

He stared at me for a long while. "Jericho," he said finally, "you never had a friend in your life. I beat my brains out trying to find just one reason besides the Bicek-Perille mess for you to be here on."

"Just one other reason, huh?"

"Yeah," Ferris said. "Just one other reason."

"How about Sanitary Blacky, Ferris? Maybe I came back for that one friend you forgot I had."

Ferris picked up his coffee cup and gulped at it. Then he watched me some more. "Maybe you did," he said. "But the same thing goes there. You stay clear of that. When I pounded a beat we didn't have any problems. I don't want any with you now. This city has had enough killings."

"You want me to lie to you, Ferris?" I asked. "Should I say I'll stay as pure as the wind-driven snow while I'm in town?"

"Just stay clear of killing trouble."

"Don't I always?" I asked. "I need a favor, Ferris. I want to talk to some old friends."

"Nobody is stopping you," he said. "Maybe two of them are looking for you now." He watched me closely and smiled. "Like Otto and Jo-Jo."

"I can't talk to my friends if I've got to spend all my time looking for them."

"So who do you want to find?"

"Who's around?"

"Do I look like an information center?" Ferris asked. "There's a thousand punks in town."

"I don't know a thousand punks."

He thought for a moment, then said, "Gonzales, T-Bone, Decker, and Greek; they're still around, of the old ones you knew. Bicek has Fendora and Gus Gogh with him."

"I don't know them," I said. "From what I've heard, he hasn't got much help."

Ferris grunted. "He's got enough help; you can add Jack Ford to that list too."

He put his cigar into his coffee cup. "For not having

much to work with, I'd say Bicek is running up one hell of a score, isn't he?"

"Is he?"

"I wish to hell I knew," Ferris said. "It's going to be a worse headache with you here." He paused. "Whose side are you on?"

I finished my coffee, and gave him an honest answer. "My own, Ferris," I said. "I didn't know there was any other one."

That was the end of our talk. Ferris had what he wanted—a good close look at me—and I had a few names I wanted. I also knew that the two hoods from Chicago wouldn't be good news for me if they had gone to Bicek.

It didn't surprise me any that Greek was still one of the living in town. He was one of the men getting bled by the rackets, which let him make just enough of the easy money to keep him paying.

I rented a car and spent the next hour driving around the West Side, until I began to wonder if I was just looking for the guts to begin again. I decided that if I wanted it right, I would need to find out how the first body had reached the morgue, and work up to Blacky and John Candoli from there. I drove down to Ninth Street, and watched my homecoming go by while I walked and smoked.

four

The city hadn't changed much; they never do. It had become a little older and shabbier, and there were some new faces around that helped dig at the mind with thoughts of the past. It could even be a bit frightening, because you'd reached a place you'd once called home, and found out that life had continued without you; people had grown older, and some had died, some had moved out to love and hate in other places, and some had fought a dirty gutter war that had helped to bring you back.

It seemed like a million years since I'd been there and though the city still looked as if it were rotting against the skyline, as it used to look to me, mixed with the familiarity was a quality of strangeness that made it easy to feel like an outsider.

It takes a while when a man comes back. He walks the old streets, drinks in the same bars, and the city reclaims him slowly, filling in the missing years until they're forgotten.

I walked for a long time in the cold rain with the streets almost deserted, and managed to wander over to James Street, where we used to hang out in a drugstore before we started stealing and acquired the necessary money to shift our hangouts over to Ninth. The kids didn't care if it was James or Ninth Street now, and you could smell the pot and heroin from the doorways where they gathered. And the young hookers, who were taking on-the-job training at sixteen, were willing to argue price with you in the rain, practicing looking sexy with their young-old faces, appearing eager as they opened cheap raincoats to show what the cheap sweaters underneath were holding. Before I returned to the car, I'd decided that most things hadn't changed much, and only a few of the people had.

I'd picked up some news since I'd gotten back. The newspaper had printed the fact that Joe Noto had been shot on Ninth Street three months ago. It figured that he'd been the first to go then, and that Greek's place was where it had begun. I headed for the bar in the rain, while I thought about Noto.

Dead or alive, there was no changing what Noto had

been, and dying with half of his face shot off, as the newspaper reported, didn't alter his having been a one hundred percent bastard—which, being a hood, had made him a handy man to have around.

Noto had been Iron Mike's man, and about as loyal as any hood is. For all his loyal service he had come through the ranks from pimp to collector, which is one advantage of belonging to a racket boss—there's room for advancement. And with Iron Mike behind him, Noto could enjoy his favorite pastime of whipping heads with little risk of having his own whipped, under ordinary circumstances. Three months ago, when Bicek moved in, the circumstances became no longer ordinary.

Greek's bar seemed like the place to start looking for John Candoli, and a killer for Blacky. Occupying two buildings off the corner of Ninth and James, it was a wooden, three-story firetrap that stacked up as the bar, rooms for the whores, and an army-cot-filled flophouse at the top where derelicts spent two bits a night to get out of the rain. Greek lived in the back of the place, and the girl who was tending bar went to get him while I waited and noticed without surprise that the dirt and the derelicts hadn't changed any.

I was surprised when Greek remembered me. He had grown older with me, but he, like his place, hadn't changed much. He was still fat. Even in cold weather he leaked sweat, and he always seemed oily wet in his bagging slacks and gray-white shirt. He stank like the bar, like unwashed bodies, and rancid food. His eyes traveled over my suit, and he knew I had money, which made him welcome me like a son, and buy me a drink, while

I bought a bottle for us to take to a booth in the rear.

"Fill me in, Greek," I said. "It's been a long time. I hear that your friend Noto isn't around anymore."

Greek filled his glass with whiskey and his eyes brightened. "That was the best thing that happened to Ninth Street in twenty years. You should have been here; all the creeps were crawling for a hole before it was over."

I poured my own whiskey and smiled at him in a way he didn't like. "You sound pleased with the new establishment, Greek. What happened, did you want a change of who you pay your protection money to? Or do you just like Bicek better than Iron Mike?"

He fumbled with his cigarettes a moment before saying, "Nothing like that, Jericho. Have you ever seen me pick sides in one of these deals?"

I shook my head. "Not yet."

"You won't either," he said, sighing. "I grease the hand of whoever is bossing things, and let it go at that. Just like every other business in this district here." He shrugged. "I've been paying that goddamn Noto for so long, I was glad to see him get it."

"Why'd he get it?"

Greek shrugged. "Collection money, I guess. He had his Friday-afternoon bag with him that day, and this is the end of his route, you know. I guess Bicek figured that there was going to be some dead boys over the takeover, so he might as well get paid for his work. He had it planned real good."

"Almost like someone had told him when and where Noto would be with the money, huh?"

"What are you trying to say?" Greek wanted to know. "You saying that I set Noto up?"

"If I had something to say, I'd say it," I told him. "Just tell me how it happened."

Greek shrugged. "You know how that lousy creep was? Like a goddamn clock he made his rounds. I could set my watch by him, so it don't take any mastermind to knock him over when he's got a bagful."

I smiled. "You're right, Greek. But it takes a little more than a gun-crazy bastard like Bicek to take over a twenty-year-old organization like Iron Mike had." I watched him for a moment. "I'm curious about that. I even have a few theories about it. But you just tell me about Noto, so I got a place to start."

Greek peered at me, and rubbed his hands on his shirt. "How much interested are you?"

"You trying to shake me down, Greek? I learned tricks up at Jeff City that will make you think Iron Mike's shakedown was a maypole dance."

"Don't get sore," he said. "You know how it is. Talking over old times takes my mind off business, and maybe I lose money."

He watched as I took a twenty from my wallet and laid it on the table. "You take a job already?" he asked.

"Let's talk about Noto."

His hand closed over the twenty and slid it off the table. "What do you want to know about that mess?"

"Start with how Noto got it."

"Sure. I'll tell you. Like I said, Friday night at seven sharp he's here. He says the same thing he says every time he walks in this place...."

"Bring it in back, Greek," Noto said. "And bring a drink in a clean glass with it."

Greek nodded reluctantly, and picked up a glass from the drain rack. He waited until Noto passed the end of the bar before he rinsed the glass out in the slop bucket and dried it carefully on his sweat-soaked shirt. Then he filled it and brought Noto his drink and thirty percent of the week's take.

"It's not so good with the girls this week," Greek said. "Maybe next week is better."

Noto grinned at him and counted the money, then said, "Maybe this week was better. Like the price of getting a broken head fixed."

Greek sighed. "Business ain't so good. I could make it up on the junk, I guess." He fished around under his apron, and put another bill on the table.

There wasn't any doubt in Greek's mind that he would make up the extra twenty on heroin. Iron Mike supplied that too. Greek cut it in half with powdered sugar, and anything else he had handy, before he passed it on to the junkies for a double rake-off. The junkies were unhappy about paying twice the price to get on cloud nine with a skinful, but who's going to kick and get cut off? It meant that they had to steal more to get to the land of dreams, but they got there.

"Mike don't say that the payoff is going to change every week," Greek said.

"I say what the payoff is in this district." Noto smiled and stared at the bar. "Where'd you get the new girl?"

"She's off the block," Greek said. "She gives me the

story her mama's sick." He shrugged. "I need another girl."

"What's she got?" Noto asked. "Clap or something?"

"What kind of a place you think I run here? Only two of my girls got a case."

"Yeah," Noto said. "And they're so goddamn ugly, you can't get more than two dollars a lay for them anyway."

"A buck is a buck," Greek said. "The creeps that want them don't worry about getting a case."

"Bastards probably got it already," Noto said. "You're a dumb bastard, Greek."

"Why do I have to be a dumb bastard?" Greek asked. "I'm a businessman."

Noto nodded at the girl. "Look at her. What's she got?"

"What have they all got at that age? Nice ass and big boobs."

"So?"

"So she looks like a good lay," Greek admitted.

Noto shook his head. "And you put her behind the bar and let the hags out here to work the customers, huh? That ain't smart, Greek. You put her out front where the boys can get a feel. Put one of the hags behind the bar."

"Maybe she don't want to work out front."

Noto stared at him and tapped a finger on the week's take. "Put her ass on the floor or get her out. You don't need any dead weight here. Now get to hell away from me so I can finish."

"So I go back to the bar," Greek told me. "And Noto's still setting right where we are with his hands in the briefcase again. It's like he don't think I see him pull a couple of bills out every Friday and put it in his own wallet. You know how much that creep must have stole from Mike—"

"Let it go," I said. "What happened?"

"I was over there in back of the bar when Bicek's boys come in."

"Who?"

"Fendora, and that dumb creep they call the Mad Dutchman."

"Louie Fendora and Gus Gogh?"

"Yeah. That's them. Anyway, they come in and walk back to the booth where he's at. And from what I've been hearing, I know they ain't here to be sociable."

Greek was enjoying his remembering now. He had seen Noto die, and he was happy to remember it for every penny of protection money he had paid out over the years. I watched him, knowing that a man like Noto is easy to hate and fear. Greek killed Noto every time he remembered the day he'd died.

"Spit it out, Greek," I said.

He wiped his mouth on his shirt sleeve and smiled. "Well, I was behind the bar like I said, and I ain't moving any. All I seen after that was them talking for a minute before Gogh shoots Noto in the face."

"Were they arguing?"

"No," Greek said. "Gogh just takes out his pistol like it's all planned, and blows Noto's head off. Hell of a mess. I had to repaint the wall after that."

"That was it then?"

"Yeah. They pick up the briefcase, and tell me that

was a message for Iron Mike and I should take my time getting to a phone." Greek took a long drink of his whiskey. "I gave them enough time to be in Alabama before I called anyone. I don't want Bicek hot at me when he plays like that."

"How did he play with John Candoli?" I asked, and watched his face. Some people twitch and stammer or just go blank when they have to field a hard lie. Greek was an old hand at the game after twenty years on Ninth Street, and he had some control. But he had never gotten around to the point where he could control his body. Like I said, he leaked sweat. I let him nurse his drink, and watched the sudden beads of sweat pop out on his forehead. He mopped his face with a gray handkerchief before he managed to ask, "Who the hell is this Candoli? I mean, where does he fit?"

"Just another thing I'm curious about," I said. "He was young, from out of town, and should have come in with the Iron Mike bunch."

Greek debated the wisdom of saying any more; then he helped himself to another shot of whiskey. "All I know is what I seen, and that was Noto."

"I think you only know what you want to," I said.

Greek considered that for a moment, and sighed. "Who in the hell wants to get mixed up in this mess, Jericho? Okay, so I heard that this Candoli was in town, and that's *all* I heard about it."

I lighted another cigarette, and sipped my drink. "Okay," I said. "What's been bothering me about this whole mess is one little thing, Greek. Sanitary Blacky. I sort of liked Blacky; so maybe you can tell me why he got pushed. Knowing him like I did, I think he would have left town before he got mixed up in this mess. So why does he wind up on a police blotter with holes in his guts?"

Greek shook his head. "Hell, Blacky was just one of those things. The cops and the newspapers got that one wrong. Bicek didn't have anything to do with him." He paused and wiped his face. "So you want to settle things for an old pal, huh?" He wiped his face again. "I know Blacky went out and made a score that night. I fenced some for him. The night he got hit he came in, passed a nice bag of hot ice to me, and then hung around with the cash. You know how Blacky was. The way I figure it is that he flashed that roll in the wrong spot that night and someone killed him for the bundle."

I grinned bleakly. "So you figure it out that he got four slugs in the stomach for his wallet, huh?"

"Yeah. Hell, yes. What else could it have been?" Greek assured me. "I gave him three hundred at ten o'clock, and that's the last time I see him alive. The cops say that he was pushed around midnight, and Christ knows where he could have been by then."

"Take a guess," I said. "Where did Blacky usually go when he was flush?"

Greek leered. "Blacky hadn't changed that much," he said. "He usually went over to see if Decker had any new girls around, or maybe Anna."

"That sounds like Blacky, all right." I dropped my cigarette butt into my glass. "I suppose Decker is one of Bicek's boys now too?"

Greek shrugged. "Who knows? I tend to business over

here. Blacky wouldn't have cared anyway. You checking on Blacky?"

I grinned at Greek until he started to sweat again. "I'm checking on a lot of things," I said. "But you can pass the word that someone is going to pay for Blacky, and I'm not real worried about who it is."

I smiled as I got up from the booth. I didn't want any more of the lies Greek had told me, and the enjoyment of watching him squirm was wearing thin.

"You're just checking on Blacky, huh, Jericho?" Greek wanted to know again.

I winked at him. "I'm checking on a lot of things, Greek. Just like I said." I nodded. "I'll be back for some more talk."

I left the bar, and drove across the river to Seventh Street. A slum in Kansas City is not any different from one in Chicago or New York. They're only different when you know them. You could go from Ninth to Seventh Street, and just the river and a sign told you that you were in another state. They were both sinkholes, and only the absence of hard booze on the Kansas side made the racket squeeze different. They both bled enough to the rackets to make them worth fighting for.

I drove past the Lighthouse Bar and its painted window and down Seventh to the stockyards, where I made a right turn along the river. I parked the car where the buildings became windowless, rotting ruins in weed-grown lots, and signs told me that the area was still waiting for the redevelopment wreckers. Even the signs were the same as when I'd left.

It was the derelicts' Shangri-La. The place where they

came when they didn't have the two bits for a flophouse, where they came when they were sick, and where the county would pick them up to bury them when they were done being sick. I had spent a few days in the backwash of the stockyards when I wanted a good place to vanish.

I sat in the car and watched the river. At its best, the Kansas River is coffee-colored, with high-water mud and debris. On the banks of Seventh Street its color is a gray black, and the current is sluggish enough to be scum-ridden and spotted with bottles and used rubbers washed down from the picnic areas above.

I watched it, and remembered. Then I got out of the car and walked along its edge. I could feel its smell like an oily smoke against my skin. I walked until the smell didn't gag me anymore and the newness of my homecoming began to ease away.

I used the time to count the lies that Greek had told me, because I knew that Blacky was too old a hand at the game to flash money where they would crowbar the poor box off the church wall. And with three hundred in his pocket, I knew Blacky would have gone to Anna's for a girl, not to Decker. I thought that maybe Greek wanted me to listen to Decker lie to me too for some reason.

But I wanted to visit one more of Bicek's boys before I did things the hard way. So I decided I would go to see Decker.

five

People can sometimes be hard to find after five years, even pimps, like Decker, who need their location known. But Decker's sideline of pushing a little dope made him drift around the city like a hot burglar. It took me three bar stops and a talk with T-Bone Slick before I picked up a line on him, and I wouldn't have found T-Bone that soon if a helpful derelict hadn't offered a few directions for a glass of rotgut and two dollars.

Derelicts have little to lose from a talk, and if you don't look too much like a cop they are eager to spread the word; all you need to be able to do is buy some wine and be willing to sort out the scattered truth in what they will tell you.

I sorted out T-Bone's address, and the fact that his vocation was still the same. He somehow managed to keep track of the action around the city, and for the right price he was willing to locate almost anyone. While I drove the rented car over to Central Avenue and legged my way up five flights of stairs to his room, I was thinking he wouldn't have much trouble finding Decker.

T-Bone was still the cautious type of guy he'd always been—at least he's the only person I know who has three night chains on the door to his pad, besides the regular snap lock, which he opened slowly to see who was in the hall. It could be that cautious was the way to be in his sort of business.

I found myself in the usual cold-water flat after the bolt scraping and chain rattling was over, and I stood there a moment while my eyes adjusted to the dimness that pulled shades caused. It took me a moment to locate T-Bone, who was hunched up like a rat in the corner chair.

"What do you need, Jericho?" he asked.

"An address for Dan Decker, to start with," I said, and listened to his dry laugh and the whisper of paper as he picked up the writing pad on the table beside him.

"You don't want much," he said. "That ain't worth making a trip over here. Anybody can find a pimp."

He came into the light and handed me the address he'd written. I studied his chalky complexion and the rotting snags in his mouth, which didn't help his grin any.

I wagged my head at him. "That's not all I want," I said, and handed him a twenty. "I want everything you can get me on Sanitary Blacky, to start with, and I want a dead-sure answer on what happened to John Candoli after he came down here."

T-Bone crawled back into his chair, and scratched the week-old stubble on his face. "It'll cost you," he said. "That's digging into Bicek's business, and I'm not doing that for less than a hundred." He pursed his lips and whistled soundlessly. "You start asking for trouble as soon as you get into town, huh? You sure you want this information?"

"I want it."

He shrugged. "I guess Blind Willie can fiddle a funeral march over your grave too, like the others lately." T-Bone picked up the notepad again and did some more writing. "When do you want this info?"

"I wanted it yesterday." I said. "How soon can you get it?"

"You got a grudge against living?" he wanted to know. "What's the rush?"

"Let's just say that I like to be sure of things and I don't like running around town without knowing who's on whose ball team." I smiled at him in the dimness. "Whose team are you playing on, T-Bone?"

He shrugged, saying, "I'm a sideliner. Where can I get you when I have something?"

I gave him my address, and got a whiff of his smile. "I

should make you pay in advance for this," he said. "But from what I see in town you can break even long enough to pay your bills, I guess."

"Thanks, sport," I told him. "I'll be around, or you'll hear about it."

"Yeah, I'll hear about it, all right." He grinned. "I usually do."

The rain outside was a relief after T-Bone's room, and I reached the street looking at the address he'd given me. Deciding that a walk across Bethany Park was easier than the drive, I left the car where it was parked and headed for Decker's place on Tenth Street. You could say that Decker was coming up in the world with that address. If being a bigger and better pimp and pusher was coming up. At least he wasn't still peddling his wares on the corner of Seventh and in the bars. If you knew a little city history, that fact told you something, because Iron Mike would never have let Decker handle enough of anything to allow him to move up on his cut of the money. Iron Mike had known that Decker was street-corner talent, and no more. And letting him move up to anything else was asking for trouble, with Decker flashing a roll, driving a Cad or such, and living high enough so that he couldn't explain his income to the cops. Knowing a little city history made me think that Decker's move to running a cat house on Tenth Street was because he had a new boss now. One he'd done some favors for, like maybe Bicek.

I walked toward Tenth Street, and kicked some thoughts about Decker around in my mind. A hood who comes up from his street corner wouldn't like to be reminded about where he came from. I was going to remind Decker, and I was sure that seeing me was going to make him start being unhappy. But he was going to tell me a few things about Bicek too, any way he wanted to do it, because just as Iron Mike had known about him, I knew that it wouldn't take too much arm twisting to make him talk. The twisting wouldn't bother me, since I wasn't loaded down with love for Decker to begin with.

There were couples on the park sidewalk with their summer raincoats and slow walks, and I sidestepped them as I hurried for the park's center path with my head bent and my jacket pulled up against the occasional cold slash of rain that was enough to keep things cold and damp; and to make me wonder why walking had seemed like a good idea.
I walked under the dripping trees at the park's edge, and remembered I'd been known to like doing stupid things before, like wet walks. I'd done a lot of it in Bethany Park with Judy, and not minded it so much then. At the center path that cuts the park into triangles between Central and Tenth, I stopped to light a cigarette, and turned my back to the wind from the river. It didn't take me long to decide that lighting that one was pulling a nail out of my coffin instead of putting one in; I saw two men in a car a half block behind me, and gauged their creep-along speed.
The tail was a hard one to miss, with the light traffic, and their trying to keep up with my walking. I took my time with the cigarette, and managed to peg the rent-a-car sticker on the bumper before I turned and went on

past the cross path toward Seventh Street.

Unless I'd gotten a bad case of nerves or paranoid in stir, it seemed that the rumble was out on one Jericho Jones. And from what I'd seen, I was pretty sure that the two in the car weren't cops, and they were nothing local in the line of guns that I knew.

I smiled as I walked, feeling safe for a moment with the rain walkers around the park, while I searched my mind for any recollection of the two in the car. I couldn't pick out anything familiar about the horse-faced driver, or the bullet-headed slob with the close-set eyes who was sitting beside him. They had only one look to me, one that I couldn't miss. They looked like guns for one of the teams playing the power-grab game, and my walking the fence between the two sides made them unhealthy to me, either way. As I crossed the street at Seventh and walked left toward the Lighthouse Bar, I knew I didn't need them on my back. We hadn't been introduced, but I was willing to bet that my slow-driving tails were Otto and Jo-Jo of Chicago, as Ferris had told me. I wasn't quite set on the idea that they were Bicek's men; there were just too many hats in the ring to tag them yet.

I pushed through the doors of the Lighthouse, wishing that I knew who they were playing for and who had put them on me that soon. I paused at the bar long enough to drop a five in front of the bartender and tell him to set up the drinks, before I headed for the toilet in the back; it would have made an Asian honey bucket smell like a health department's dream.

The health I was worried about didn't depend on the

smell of the place at that moment. Instead it depended on my two tails not knowing the city like I did, and being reluctant to split their team. I pushed open the door leading to the alley and glanced out at the litter and piled bottles that decorated the narrow brick passage leading toward the stockyards. I could have kept going and lost my tail in the rain and the twist of alleys, I suppose. Only doing that would still leave them around and I wanted them to know that playing bird dog in my back yard could be unhealthy. So I picked up an empty fifth from the pile beside the door and, leaving the alley door open, walked back up the evil-smelling hall and stood behind the open door to the can.

    I was remembering that it was a good way to get myself buried, about the time I heard Otto and Jo-Jo hurrying down the hall. They were pros enough about the business to figure that the open alley door meant they had lost me; they would figure like that because they were used to having people run from them. And they would have expected anything out there in the alley. But they didn't expect me to step out of the reeking can behind them and tell Otto hello as I smashed the whiskey bottle over his right temple, and peeled an inch-wide strip of skin off his bald head as the bottle broke.

    Otto was no problem at all after that. He just flopped over against the wall, slid quietly down, and rolled over like a dead hog while he bled onto the stinking floor. Jo-Jo wasted a few seconds watching him do that before his hand snaked up under his jacket. I needed that few seconds to get to him before his hand could get back out with the .45 he was digging for. He had a long, bony face and yellow eyes that went expressionless as my fist smashed into his throat. He gagged some until I bounced his head off the wall and then I kicked him in the jaw, sending him down on the floor to keep Otto company. I watched the two for a long time before I checked their wallets and took Jo-Jo's .45 with me back out into the rain. I knew two things about the pair then: their not having identification made them contract men, and the John Doe names on their drivers' licenses made them Chicago boys. I also knew that there was only one way I was going to get them off my back, and I didn't need the fresh body of one of them to put Ferris on my back in their place. I felt Jo-Jo's .45 pressed against my stomach, and wondered when they'd try me again to earn their money. They would be more careful then.

Thinking like that didn't improve my mood any by the time I reached Decker's place. A sleepy-sounding voice told me to come on in.

The apartment had the usual worn furnished-room look, with stained tan wallpaper, cracked plaster, and the floor showing through the rug. The air-conditioner in the window and a portable bar were Decker's only homey touches. He was making use of the bar supplies near the window where he sat, and he smiled an automatic smile when he told me to make myself a drink and have a seat.

Decker was heavier than he'd been five years ago, and his hairline had migrated to the top of his head as the hair was turning gray. But the flat face and hooked nose hadn't changed, and his hands still shook from too much booze.

He waved a glass to take in the room and said, "Quite a change, huh? Not like that hole I used to have."

"You're doing all right, Decker," I said. "Business must be good."

He watched me, then glanced around the room. "I get by," he said. "What's on your mind?"

"Sanitary Blacky's on my mind," I said softly. "So is Iron Mike, and a few others." I waited a minute and smiled. "Who are *you* working for these days?"

He shrugged. "I'm like the rest. I pay the man on top. What the hell's the difference—Bicek or Iron Mike?"

"Blacky didn't pay either one of them," I said. "Why did he get pushed?"

"I hear he got rolled," Decker said quickly. "Nothing to do with Bicek."

"Tell that to the cops, Decker; maybe they'll believe you. I think that somebody wanted Blacky out of the way. It makes me wonder why."

Decker set his glass down. "Maybe you shouldn't wonder so much about that. Things have changed around this town. Bicek's running things."

"Bicek's a punk who couldn't make a whorehouse pay on an army post," I said. "Things haven't changed that much. But maybe I should talk to him about Blacky; seeing as he's the big man now."

"He ain't afraid of you, Jericho," Decker said. "He's got some important friends around too."

"Sure," I said. "And who have you got, Decker? You got friends like you have guts, and those run down your leg when you walk on a dark street." I leaned forward in the chair and smiled at him. "You want to tell me about all the big connections *you* have? Or would you rather just answer a few questions?"

Decker shook his head. "It ain't healthy to talk to you, man. I don't want any trouble. It ain't healthy to talk around this town at all."

"It isn't healthy *not* to talk to me," I said. "I'm here and Bicek isn't."

"Look," Decker said hurriedly. "There ain't a thing I can tell you about Blacky. He didn't buy any ass here."

"Tell me about Candoli then," I suggested.

He shook his head again quickly. "You're talking to the wrong man; I just pay my bills. I got nothing to do with Bicek and that business."

"Sure, Decker," I said, watching him. "You just run a whorehouse and push dope; you wouldn't know what the big kids are doing, would you?"

I could feel Decker's hate in the room as he sat and watched me. I smiled at him and thought about being lied to every time John Candoli's and Blacky's names came up. I didn't think I'd learn anything about either one of them from Bicek's people. It seemed like a good time to start looking for a few of the people that Bicek was unpopular with, and I hoped that Otto and Jo-Jo didn't turn out to be some of those. That was another little item that needed an answer: just who was paying two of Chicago's talent for tailing me? That didn't fit either, unless Candoli had sent them to protect his investment in me. There wasn't a lot of trust connected to a contract like mine. It helped to remind me that you couldn't really be sure who was behind what, which makes you careful. It also made me enjoy sitting in the apartment with Decker and watching him squirm while he hated.

I was feeling the sourness of the day inside me and the routine of the past creeping back, when Decker showed the mood he was in as he barked in response to a knock on the door. He needed something to take his hate out on, and for him the hustlers he owned were ideal for that.

When you've lived with hustlers, you can recognize a pro from an amateur at a glance, but it was only Connie Hunt's fear of Decker, which showed in her face, that made me watch with interest as she walked into the room. She looked like the kind of girl who would fail her pimp a lot of times before she resolved herself to the trade. She wore the usual cheap cotton dress of Decker's girls, and a fresh look that even her fear couldn't hide. She was a country girl in the city to do great things, and she'd learned that she couldn't do anything but sell herself or return to the country. She was tall, almost my own height in heels, and she wore her red hair long and loose. She had a lithe body that would make money in the right places once she had gotten through the stage of breaking in to twenty-dollar amateur harlotry. Her green eyes went with the red hair, and I enjoyed watching her, because I'd always had a thing for redheads; at least I had a thing for any redhead that Decker owned.

She hesitated a moment when she saw me, and glanced at Decker.

"Give me the money and get to hell out," he told her. "I'll see you later."

"I don't have it," she said.

Decker didn't forget about me; he was too eager to prove what a big man he was. There was a pinched grin on his flat face when he said, "What do you mean you haven't got it? Don't hold out on me, bitch."

"He didn't pay," she said simply. "Did you want me to call the cops when he walked out?"

Decker came out of the chair, showing his crooked smile to me while his fingers dug into the redhead's arm. "How about that, Jericho? She wants to hustle and ain't got enough sense to get paid before she gets laid."

"Please," she whispered, and pulled away from him.

"Stupid hick-town bitches," Decker said as he slapped her. He slapped like a man hitting a punching bag that he knows won't hit back, doing it slowly and with enjoyment as she twisted and grew crimson with the slaps. She cried because it hurt, but she didn't beg, and when she looked at me she didn't ask for help. She stood there and took it, and only her eyes pleaded.

I let my hand settle on Jo-Jo's .45 under my belt and said, "Let her go, Decker."

He didn't. He held on and kept slapping, saying, "Stay out of this, damn you."

I've been known to do just that. I could have walked away and it wouldn't have bothered me any longer than most things. Only Decker wasn't number one on my popularity list, and I wanted something to let a little of my own sourness out on. I wanted Decker to tell his new boss that I didn't like his disciples. So I did the same thing that Decker was doing: I found myself a dog to beat on, and pounded him into the wall with the .45.

The redhead stopped me before Decker had any more

than a split in his scalp and was spending his time holding his head while he crouched on the floor. It helped some to know that when he went to Bicek he would be sure I hadn't believed him.

I walked out of the apartment remembering the redhead standing there, watching Decker hold his face and do the whimpering for a change, and was outside on the sidewalk when she caught up with me, carrying a small overnight bag in her hand.

"Wait a minute," she said. "I can't stay here."

"Patch him up and he'll love you," I said. "Tell him you saved him from a trip to the hospital."

"I know. I just can't—"

"Where do you want to go?" I asked. "With your equipment you can always find another pimp."

She colored slightly as I looked at her, watching the wind move her hair around her face.

"Let me go with you," she said. "Just for a few days."

I looked her over again, starting with the slender legs and working my way up to the way her breasts pressed against the too-small dress. When my eyes reached hers again, she took a deep breath that stretched the dress top, and surveyed me speculatively as she stepped closer. "You like?" she asked.

"I like," I said. "Only I've got a credit card for a whorehouse and I'm not taking up pimping."

"This is cheap though," she said. "You provide the place, and I'll provide the bed company." She hooked her arm through mine, pressing against my arm. "Please," she added. "Just for a few days."

She stood there watching me while I decided that

there wasn't any question in there being advantages to having her around. She'd sleep with me, and I'd have someone to talk to besides myself. And it had been a long time since I'd enjoyed talking to myself.

"Is that all you have?" I asked, nodding at the small bag she carried.

"I left what he gave me."

"All right, redhead," I told her. "The car's on the other side of the park. Let's go get something to eat, and we'll talk about it."

We found the car and a place to eat and we didn't talk about it. There was nothing to talk about when we both knew the apartment sharing would last until she decided to move, or I decided not to come back. There never is much to talk about when you live out of a suitcase, and fantasy is the way people live uptown, where living together lasts more than a few weeks.

I relaxed some with her during lunch, and realized that she was easy to talk to because she wasn't an old memory or part of anything that I had to do. Connie was twenty years old, and had been born on a badland farm that had blown away every hot summer. It had killed her parents, who had tried to make a go of a bad thing, and left her to live with an uncle until a year after his wife had died, when she'd decided that the bright lights of the city were better than being pawed by a lonesome old man. The city proved to her that there were a lot of young men around who wanted to do the pawing. She'd run out of a job and money, and started charging for the pawing privileges.

She told the story placidly, and it was an old one with

a thousand variations. I didn't quite believe it, but she didn't act as if she had expected much else from a place where a sixteen-year-old could be a pimp. She'd be as well off as any of us after she learned to work the uptown clubs, where the johns paid more for what she had to offer.

I left it at that, and bought her some clothes during the afternoon to get her out of Decker's sheath before I took her back to my apartment to find out what she did have to offer.

With the rain and wind it was cool in the apartment, and we'd brought along a fifth to help the evening along. Connie was already pouring drinks after inspecting the kitchen, when I came back from dropping the .45 off in the bedroom. She carried the glasses across the room, handed one to me, and asked, "Was Blacky Shaw a close friend of yours? I mean, he must have been for all the trouble you could get into."

I grinned. "I knew him. And Decker isn't any trouble like his boss might be. How did you know about Blacky anyway? Customer or something?"

Connie shrugged. "Not while I was there, or at least not one of mine. I heard Decker mention both of your names while he was talking on the phone last night."

"Talking to Bicek maybe?"

"I don't know." She shook her head. "He just said that you'd make trouble over Blacky Shaw. That was before I met you, so I didn't pay much attention. I don't know if it was Bicek or someone else that he was talking to."

"I was told that Blacky sometimes came over to see one of Decker's girls."

She turned and looked at me. "If he was seeing one, it must have been away from the house," she said. "Maybe Decker was sending one of the girls out to him, only that's more expensive."

I shook my head. "Blacky wasn't fussy," I told her. "But he always went over to another place we knew." I paused a moment. "What do you know about the Bicek and Perille mess?"

"Practically nothing, since I didn't know either one. I remember the other one you mentioned; Candoli you called him. He was a pretty good-looking guy to find sitting around Decker's, compared to the usual trade we got. I think that he was there just once." She shrugged, and tried to laugh, then almost finished her drink in one swallow. "What was at Decker's that he'd want?"

"Guess," I said sarcastically.

"Well, he never came back anyway," she said. "I suppose if he wanted to get laid he could find a better place to—oh, hell."

"Don't let it get you down, redhead," I told her. "You've got all the equipment in the right places. You'd do all right in any place."

"Sure," she said. "Let's skip it, huh? I know what I am." She curled up on the couch and leaned against me. "That's all I can tell you about that bunch. I wasn't there to take notes, you know."

"I know," I said. "At least I know that Decker was sure I'd make trouble over Blacky."

"He's important to you?"

"Not as important as money. He was a friend, so I'll check that out while I'm here."

82

She thought that over. "It doesn't sound healthy, doing that. Is a friend that important?"

"The pay is good on the other job," I said. "I can afford to do Blacky a favor because I think he's connected to Candoli somehow. That's the one I want to find."

"What if he's dead too?"

"That's the name of the game. I get paid to find out answers like that." I watched her face. "And sometimes I get paid to do something about it."

"It's none of my business," she said, and tried to smile. "But I know what they say about you anyway."

"Spare me the details."

She shivered and picked up her glass, then finished her drink before she slid both of her arms around my neck. "We're all something," she said. "It doesn't matter to me what you are."

"That's nice," I said, and she cut off my words with her mouth, while her body moved deliberately against me. I wasted several moments thinking that I still had enough of the night left to visit Ninth Street again, and maybe talk to Greek about some lies he'd handed me. And then I wasted some more time remembering that there had been a lot of dying going on that nobody had any good answers for. The rain made it sound like it was a good night for dying out there, so I said to hell with it, and pulled Connie tight to me.

Tomorrow was soon enough for the rest.

six

Thursday morning was without rain, a clear day that came with an early sun to bake the city dry in a growing heat that could be felt through the shaded windows of the apartment when I awoke.

Connie viewed the whiskey and soda in the kitchen cabinets as something less than housekeeping supplies, and moved around the room restlessly while I dressed to take her out to breakfast.

We found a greasy spoon on the corner, and as we ate I told her that I had things to do around the city. She didn't ask what or where. Instead she said, "I can cook, and clean the apartment, and take care of the laundry —things like that."

"What for?" I wanted to know. "We made a deal. You're sleeping with me. I don't expect you to be the hired girl."

"Maybe I just expect to take care of the apartment of the man I'm sleeping with," she said. "Or I can work the bars downtown—I could pay my own way then." She closed her eyes for a moment, then added, "You don't need any dead weight around."

I winked at her. "After last night I don't think I've got any." I thought about her working the bars and, not liking the idea, gave her some money to stock the apartment with domestic supplies, if that was what she wanted. She was smiling over her coffee when I went out into the day's heat to call Greek.

"Where's Speedy Gonzales and Anna Ryan at now, Greek?" I asked.

"You looking for a Mexican and a whorehouse this early in the day?"

"Anna still running the same house?"

"Yeah. Hell yes. What do you think the fancy old bitch would be doing? Knitting?"

"How about Gonzales?"

"Still down at that hole he calls a bar," Greek said. "He won't be there long if he don't start paying off though."

"He's not paying Bicek, you mean?"

"So they tell me," Greek said. "He'll be a *real* wetback if he keeps it up. One with cement blocks tied to his legs when he hits the river."

"Save your comedy for the customers," I told him. "Just give me the address."

I wrote it down, listening to his voice over the wire. "You know this is a goddamn stupid way to spend your time, don't you?"

"Sure," I agreed. "But I'm queer for spending my time in stupid ways; it upsets people. I'll see you around," I added, and hung up the phone while I checked my watch. Nine o'clock in the morning may be too early to visit a whorehouse, as Greek had said, but it wasn't too early to see Gonzales. According to Greek's information, Speedy might be the only one around who would give me any straight information from Iron Mike's side of that fence I was walking.

It took me forty-five minutes of driving along the river section below the stockyards to reach Gonzales' bar. I wasn't sightseeing, since I knew what that section of the city looked like too, and there was little to see in the garbage-filled alleys and overgrown vacant lots. It was the part of the city where you lived if your skin was the wrong color, no matter what the NAACP preached. It's where grass grows in the cracks of the sidewalk, and where flats, walk-ups, and brownstones are weathered paint-free and sooted with factory smoke until they stand like decaying teeth. The familiarity was there, right down to the hard-faced cop who had two sullen-faced men spread-eagled against a building while he searched them, and a slack-jawed derelict perched on the curb watching the shakedown with vacant-eyed interest. It was like watching a rerun on TV and, like the first showing, it wasn't getting through to me. I drove on, hoping that something Speedy told me would get through, and things would start to add up.

Speedy Gonzales was like Greek, a front owner for a bar that the rackets pulled the profits from. Iron Mike used to pocket the Lucky Sombrero and, according to Greek, Speedy wasn't eager to start paying off any new racket boss.

Speedy was a numb little immigrant who used booze to try to stay numb. He came from El Centro in the sunny south as a kid, crossing the border early in life to find the land of many pesos, where he'd been told that all men were equal. He reached Kansas City thirty years ago to learn the sad truth the hard way, and now felt fortunate to be able to earn a living at all—even in the rackets. Speedy was fifty-two years old, and a look at his thin frame made a person think that he must have a moonlight job, like being referee for wildcat fights. And when you get right down to it, running a bar like the Lucky Sombrero was equivalent to that when there was a barful of migrant workers well primed with rotgut and sharp knives.

The bar was cool, empty, and stinking from old booze like any other dive when I entered and sat down across from Speedy. He gave me a mild smile of recognition, and set a bottle on the bar between us while we made small talk. I waited until the bottle was three-quarters gone, and Speedy was comfortably numb, before I said, "What's this I hear about you not going for the new payoff arrangements around town? Don't you like Bicek?"

"I don't like any of them, Jericho, why should I? But

I pay to Iron Mike for thirty years here." He shrugged. "I don't like how it's going now, so I don't pay anybody until I see who's boss. Only Bicek tells me that he is."

"That's what they say."

"Maybe he isn't though. There was one of Mike's people I don't know about."

"An out-of-town boy—like from Chicago maybe?" I asked. "A good-looking guy, black hair and a go-to-hell grin?"

"How should I know Chicago, Jericho? I know this one is out-of-town, and Mike's man. He looked like you say."

"Could his name have been Candoli?"

"Something like that maybe."

"Why do you think that he might be around yet, with Mike dead? And how in hell can you figure him for taking over now?"

Speedy stared through me for a moment, then held up the almost empty bottle. I took the hint and pushed a ten across the bar. "Look," Speedy said. "Rackets I been around for a long time, right? I know who it takes to run them. I tell you that this Candoli guy was a guy that could. He even ran Iron Mike's meeting here."

"What meeting?"

"They hold a meeting here after Noto gets killed—all of Mike's people—to decide what they do about Bicek."

"And John Candoli was there?"

"He's here. He's here like he's running things, and he does just what Mike doesn't need then. I think later that maybe this Candoli is on his own side, and screws Bicek and Mike both. Now I wait to see who turns up as boss."

"I hear that Candoli is dead too," I said, and waited.

"No bodies turned up. Nothing has been in the newspapers. Why should I pay to Bicek until I'm sure?" Speedy said, and left it there.

He was like every bar boss caught in a syndicate squeeze. He didn't want to wind up paying two bosses at once. And he had thirty years of rackets and booze behind him to help make him stubborn enough to wait Bicek out right to the limit.

"Tell me about the meeting here when Candoli was in."

Speedy sighed, picked up the new bottle, and led me to a back booth before he started telling me about Iron Mike's disciples, who had sat around the bar, looking tired and unhappy because they didn't want to get up early and listen to some out-of-town talent tell them how to run a war with Bicek.

The one kill-by-contract man of the bunch was a Mexican with the tag of Black Maria, and he'd had more reason than the rest to be unhappy with the early-morning meeting, because he'd had to leave his seventeen-year-old whore while he listened to Candoli. Knowing Black Maria, I could see his point; he didn't trust strangers. He didn't trust his seventeen-year-old whore either.

He had reached his present station in life by not trusting anyone. He was a shifty-looking, medium-size man, with an odd walk that reminded people of the sidestepping walk of a crab. He also had the temper of a sick junkie, and was about as psychopath as they come. Myself, I'd trust him enough to let him blink twice at me before I put a bullet above his belt; that was the only thing Black Maria would understand. He'd put enough men away to make him dangerous, and he knew the rules. He used to run a section of the city for Iron Mike, and had been called a wetback like Speedy, but the only river he'd ever crossed was between the two cities.

He had run his section of the city for Mike with the expert pleasure of a man who likes to use a shiv, and one who likes to hurt before he kills by contract. I would have called him the best Mike had, and knew enough to respect his ability, and because he enjoyed his work enough to get his kicks from it he was content with local jobs. He would have gotten a step up the racket ladder sooner or later. All he needed to do was to keep on cutting the people Mike wanted cut, and he'd have been a big man.

Another of Mike's disciples at the meeting was Jack Ford. He wanted to help Maria become a big man, with the hidden hope that he'd get himself killed, and then Ford could screw Maria's whore in safety. Ford ran the Parish Street section for Mike. He was a tired-looking hood with a flabby face and food stains on his shirt. His one hope of going anyplace in the rackets, or any business, was that all the young men had accidents. He played the young, eager hoods in Mike's crew against one another and hoped for better days and things—like a piece of Black Maria's girl.

The rest of the disciples at the meeting would have liked a piece too, when they thought about it, because she was the hottest little barnstorming stripper in town, in Speedy's view. But at the meeting, the group would just as soon have gone back to bed as listen to Candoli try to impress them with the Candoli name, and other big ideas.

John Candoli had surprised all of them that day by walking in and ordering everyone a drink. He even surprised Speedy, by paying for it. After that, I gathered from Speedy's account, the meeting had gone like a class-B Capone movie—though I doubt that Speedy had ever seen a Capone movie.

Jack Ford made the introductions, and then bought another round with Candoli's money while the imported talent told the gathered disciples that he was running things.

Nobody thought Mike would like that.

"Mike hopes you don't like it," Candoli told them. "Better yet, *I* hope you don't like it." He paused. "Anybody here that don't like it?"

"He wants to know if we don't like it," Ford said.

"I don't like it," Black Maria told him.

The rest of the group kept their mouths shut, and worked at their whiskey.

"Fine," Candoli said. "What don't you like about it?"

"Any of it," Black Maria said, and put his hand into the pocket where he kept his shiv.

Candoli looked around the room, smiled, then asked, "How bad do we need this wetback?"

"I ain't a wetback."

"Take your hand out of your pocket," Candoli advised.

Black Maria looked around the room and took his hand out, flicking the blade of his knife into the light.

"That's bad," Ford said. "There's no call to pull a knife."

Candoli smiled and pulled his .38 free from his belt holster, causing Speedy Gonzales to duck behind the bar, and the rest of the disciples to crawl under the tables.

"You're a smart wetback, ain't you?" Candoli asked.

"I think maybe you're right," Black Maria agreed. "I like things the way you like things. Everybody is one big happy family against that Bicek bastard, okay?"

"Put the knife away," Candoli said.

Black Maria put it away and shrugged, thinking about his whore. "*Sí,*" he said. "I make a joke."

"*Sí,*" Candoli said, smiling. "But I'm not joking." He proved that by shooting Black Maria in the stomach.

Maria sat down on the floor and held his belly. "You crazy bastard," he said, watching his guts leak out around his fingers.

"*Sí,*" Candoli said, and shot him again.

According to Speedy, after that it was a Candoli meeting. I thought about it, trying to put the story together, while he went behind the bar for another bottle.

Nothing fit.

I had considered the possibility of Candoli's coming to town and trying to take over Mike's action. But he'd logically want to get rid of Bicek first. So it made sense to try to keep as many of Mike's good men for that work as he could. Black Maria had been good at that work, so killing him didn't make sense.

But Sanitary Blacky's death didn't make any sense either, I remembered, and asked Speedy about that. It was a question that got me exactly nothing, just like questions about John Candoli's being in the river did.

I tossed off my drink and pushed my hat back. "Well, was it possible that Candoli was willing and eager to shoot Maria over a bit of fluff? Maria's girl?"

"What isn't possible, Jericho? I hear that Candoli took her out of Maria's place after that. But I haven't heard anything about her since. I think that she stayed with him until after Mike got killed and Bicek started to move in. After that..." He made a doubtful motion with his hands. "Hell, who worries about a piece of fluff then? There was too muck killing going on around here to be worried about a shack-up."

"If she was stripping at seventeen, it had to be in a racket-owned bar," I said. "Which one was it?"

Speedy grinned. "At the Blackstone."

I nodded. "She must have had a good thing going to work there," I said absently, knowing that the hotel-bar was a sort of snob-hill spot for the local fast-handed politicians and the unionized brotherhood of thugs, like the ones who paid my bills. It was a place for Syndicate bigwigs and the city's social set who rubbed shoulders with them.

I got the girl's name from Speedy—Lora Franks—and brooded about the little there was to learn where Bicek was concerned. Finally I shook my head, and left Speedy to his numbing process while I went back out into the heat. I was liking the smell of the contract less and less, because looking for Candoli wasn't working out in the pattern of a usual manhunt. You can usually find a man by talking to his friends, or to the people who hate his guts; one of the groups will always drop some lead to work with. All I wanted to find out just now was if Candoli was dead; and even there I was drawing blanks from both sides. A sensible guy would have put an RIP in front of Candoli's name and let it go at that. A sensible guy would have said, "All right, you dumb son-of-a-bitch, let's cross Candoli off the list and figure him for the river." That easily done bit of rationalizing would have left me free to pocket ten thousand bucks and start paying more attention to the who-shot-Blacky-Shaw game. Only there had to be someone in the city who knew how and where Candoli had got it—if he had—just as there had to be someone who knew *why* Blacky had got it. There were just too damn many *if* and *why* questions to the contract to keep me happy. I sat in the hot car and waited for an idea to creep around.

No idea came, which proved that I didn't have any great future in the art of deduction, and it was beginning to look like I'd have to do what I'd told Decker, and pay Bicek a visit. It wasn't a happening I was looking forward to, I decided. It was one I'd save for last, since I still had Anna and Lora Franks to see. There wasn't any doubt that they would be better company than Bicek.

The heat in the car dulled all thought. It hung in the air like a hot Turkish towel, and glued my suit jacket to my back with sweat. It was too hot for anything but a cold bottle, and I had just decided that it was too bad I couldn't earn my money like that, and started the car, when Speedy came out of the bar, looked at me doubtfully, and handed me a piece of paper.

"She called a few minutes ago and said that Greek told her you were maybe here." He paused, started to say something more, then shrugged and went back into the bar, while I sat and stared at Judy's name and address on the scrap of paper he'd left.

I closed my eyes and drifted back five years in the heat, remembering the sleepless nights in the cell block when I'd counted the bars and thought about how it would feel to have a woman. The old thoughts of Judy were something I couldn't shake off, and they brought back the gut-sick feeling I'd had on the night I'd walked into the apartment and caught her in bed with company.

What I'd done had been a mistake. A pro had no room for allowing his feelings to interfere with his business, and getting myself five years was a stupid way to settle something that I could have walked out on. I'd told myself for a long time that I'd only taken the risk because her bed companion had sold me out, and I knew it was a weak lie to hand even myself.

I studied Judy's address for a moment before I pulled away from the curb, and headed the car toward her apartment thinking that I could kill some past ghosts this time. The apartment building was a six-story job with a new front and a clean smell about it. I checked the mailboxes until I found Judy's name under apartment 56, and fingered the row of buttons until I was buzzed through the second door and into the lobby.

As I headed for the elevators I glanced casually around the cool, carpeted room and took in the well-oiled and polished appearance of the place. It was a cinch that Judy wasn't enjoying all the carpets, mirrors, and marble floors the place had by pounding a typewriter for someone. But then I hadn't figured that she was going to stop her hustle when I'd gone up. I wondered who her steady was now.

I reached her apartment and pushed the door buzzer. Standing in the cool hallway, I remembered how it had been for us, and when the door opened I realized how well the years had treated Judy. She hadn't changed. She was small and fresh-looking, with a pile of blond hair that tumbled to her shoulders to frame her face. In her smallness there was nothing delicate. From her oval face to the familiar swell of her hips under the slightly damp bathrobe she wore, she looked completely capable of handling anything that came her way.

I looked and remembered.

Her eyes were as expressionless as her fixed smile as she said, "Jericho, you did come."

"Why not?" I asked. "Five years ago is water under the bridge." I paused and enjoyed the view the damp bathrobe was giving me. "Maybe I figured on a free one for homecoming, and came for that."

She jerked her head and smiled as she moved aside. "Come on in. You can never tell what will happen."

She said it like she already knew what would happen, and managed to show me a long stretch of leg while she closed the door and walked to the couch.

I waved a hand at the room. "All right, I'm here. Now what's it all about and who told you that I was out?"

She kept her smile and perched on the arm of the couch, where I'd have the best view. "Everybody knows you're in town," she said. "And maybe I wanted to see you for old times' sake."

I watched her, and wasn't sure that I didn't feel sorry

for her. She had always lived to be on the winning side, the side that she could see mink coats and a big house connected to. And she'd been listening to the rumors since I'd come back. They made her willing to face the humiliation of admitting that she'd screwed it up five years ago. She was thinking I could make a good thing out of the town with just Bicek left to run it.

At least that's what I figured she was thinking.

But it wasn't hard to be unpleasant with her after those years of remembering. It was easy, in fact, when I thought about her willingness to switch bed partners because it had looked like someone else was going to come out on top five years ago. And now maybe it looked to her like I might come out on top, and I wanted it clear that she wasn't going to be there with me. I also wanted to know what she could tell me about the city, if I could get them both.

I said, "Old times, huh? I remember a few old times myself, kid. I remember a nice little blond dish who didn't want to take any chances on not being with the winning side because that's where all the money was likely to be. I've often wondered what sort of a story that kid handed you to make you think his selling me out was going to get him someplace. All it would have gotten him was dead."

She licked her lips and adjusted the bathrobe. "That's water under the bridge, remember? Dead history, huh?"

"Yeah," I said. "So let's bring up some live history. Like I wonder if your friend would like our little meeting."

"My—friend?"

"Your jocker who's paying the rent here; like *I* used to pay the rent. Think he'd go for this old-friend business?"

"Don't be crude."

"It's one of my talents. I know that whoever you're shacking up with wouldn't like my being here. And I know that you must want something to risk losing all of this sweet setup." I nodded toward the cigar butt in the ashtray. "Whoever smokes those won't like our visit, or was it his idea?"

"He doesn't know," she said. "But he wouldn't care."

"That's the story of the year, Judy. He's willing to share his stock, huh? I wonder what he wants in return." I shook a cigarette from the pack on the table and smiled at her. "Do I know him?"

"It doesn't matter," she said, and crossed her legs.

I shrugged. "You're right about that anyway. Now what do you want?"

She moved to the chair across from me, and sat down. "It's the other way around." She smiled. "What do *you* want?"

I watched her.

"What do you want in town?" she asked, letting the robe fall open again.

"I'll think of something," I said. "I've already had everything you can offer."

She shrugged. "You'll still like it when we get around to that. My friend—the one who pays the rent here—says your being in town doesn't have to be trouble."

"And you don't want me in trouble, is that it? All for old times' sake, huh? Your loyalty is touching, Judy." I grinned at her. "You must be in nice and tight with the fat rats in town now, but you always had a way of taking care of yourself."

"You're a crude bastard," she said sweetly.

"You said that once. Now is your jocker behind this little talk, or is it you? What do you want?"

"I never forgot you, Jericho. I could fix you up with something nice in town here. People owe me favors."

"Like what could you fix me up with?"

"Maybe certain people need a man like you on their side."

"Who are these certain people? Bicek maybe? You know better than that, Judy. I don't sell my gun twice on the same job."

"A cheap credo in your business."

"Sure, but the only one I've got, and it keeps me alive."

She smiled. "These friends of mine—maybe they're on the same side."

"Too bad your friends don't have any names," I said. "Everybody in town is singing the same song. They want to know why I'm here, but nobody wants to sing any tune I'd like to hear."

She moved lightly out of the chair and began to pace. "My friend says you're here on a contract—"

"That's not the right tune." I cut her off. "I want to hear some news about Blacky and a guy named Candoli."

She glanced quickly at me. "I don't know them."

"Same old tune." I sighed. "Why is everyone worried about me being in town? Do you think I'm the jealous love back to knock off your new playmate or something?

I'll tell you how it is, honey. You're good in bed, but not worth killing over. Your new playmate is safe."

She paused a moment, then continued to pace. "Bicek then?"

"What's he to you? A customer?"

"I'm not selling anymore."

"Well now," I said. "You *do* have an in with the big kids, don't you?" I grinned at her. "But don't worry, my business in town doesn't include any rerun with you like five years ago."

"I wish I could be sure," she said.

I took the cigarette from my mouth and started to grind it out in the ashtray. She was standing in front of me when she said again, "I really wish I could be sure."

I caught the change in the tone of her voice and glanced up in time to see the robe open. I let the show go on, and stared at her body when I should have been watching her hands. There was a derringer in her right hand when it came out of the pocket of her robe.

I stood up slowly, taking in the twin barrels of the gun, and I managed to grin.

"You still think I'm after your jocker, huh?"

Her mouth was twisted and tight over her teeth as she said, "I think so. You did it once."

"Don't give yourself that much credit."

"There's other reasons," she said, keeping the twin barrels trained on my chest.

"Like I might screw up a good thing for you and your friends, huh?" I asked, and stood up.

"Stay still, Jericho," she said, the tight little smile still on her face. "I know how to use this."

I was going to tell her that the .22 she was holding wasn't going to stop me. And that I had a big bastard of a .45 in my belt that I'd still be able to use if she shot. But I just grinned at her and said, "Now I *am* going to take you to bed, Judy. I'm going to make sure that your jocker knows you couldn't talk me out of anything, and that you aren't his private stock anymore."

I watched her hand as I started toward her, not expecting the sharp double crack when she pulled the trigger, and the sudden slash of pain in my arm and chest. The shock staggered me for a moment, and I saw the blood start to soak my shirt front before I jerked the empty gun from her hand and shoved her against the wall.

She shook her head, saying, "You're going to kill me."

I pushed her toward the bedroom. "Not unless I do it in bed," I told her. "I'll leave your jocker to do that. He's not going to like it at all when he comes home."

Later, I watched her, slumped against a chair in the bedroom, staring at the slaughterhouse look the bed had. I threw a fifty-cent piece onto the bed and said, "Tell your jocker to use that and buy himself a good piece of ass. You're not much good as bait."

"You seemed to enjoy it, you bastard," she mumbled.

"I needed someone to bandage the holes," I told her as I went out. "You were even lousy at that."

I didn't realize how right I'd been until I reached the car and felt the grayness creeping into my mind as the bleeding began again under my jacket.

It was like driving on the edge of darkness all the way to my apartment. And nothing made sense when I reached it, and called Connie.

seven

When you're carrying two new holes in your shoulder, it doesn't matter after a while, when the shock begins to wear off, what caliber gun put them there. You bleed a lot, and you hurt; that's two things all slugs have in common. If you're hit right, you bleed like hell while you hurt. I knew I'd been hit right within a few hours after my visit to Judy's apartment, and I also knew that the fun wasn't over, because the lead had to come out. It wasn't a pastime I thought I'd enjoy spending a Thursday afternoon at.

It's not simply a matter of a fast ride to the nearest hospital and turning yourself over to a starched and pressed eager young doctor. You don't do that, because doctors make nice little reports to the cops when they extract lead, or fool with bullet holes, and you do not need ninety days in the slammer while the cops ask questions about who made the bullet holes, as they keep insisting that you're locked up for your own protection.

So you deal with bullet holes the way Connie and I dealt with them. You find yourself on a kitchen table staring up at a bare light bulb as your own kind of doctor lays out the tools from his portable abortion kit, then probes around the new raw-lipped holes you've acquired.

Rolf Mattlocks is my kind of doctor. I watched him scratch the two-day stubble on his chin and stare at Connie across the table as she asked, "How bad is it?"

"Not good. Just one slug is in there yet. But the one that went through his arm cut a vein." He touched the pressure pads around my arm and peered at my face. "Can you hear me, Jericho?"

I nodded.

"Okay. One is easy, the slug is right against the bone. The other one is going to take some cutting so I can put that vein back together before you bleed to death. You want me to go ahead?"

"He needs a hospital," Connie said.

Mattlocks nodded. "You want a hospital, Jericho?"

I blinked my eyes and stared at Mattlocks. He'd been a doctor once, at least he had been one until he took a liking to drugs, and wrote too many prescriptions for nonexisting patients. He'd been put out of practice and had learned that there was a marked shortage of working doctors in other circles, and that the underworld didn't much give a damn if he had a monkey on his back as big as King Kong, or a lousy bedside manner. His new patients were even willing to make sure that he didn't run short of the stuff he once bootlegged prescriptions for.

"Can you fix it here?" I wanted to know.

He shrugged. "I've patched them before," he said. "It's your choice."

"Go ahead," I mumbled. "Do it here."

He did it there on the kitchen table, while I watched the single light bulb above us, and Connie's face. And that time I was lucky because Mattlocks had a supply of his own form of pain killer, so we didn't need to depend on whiskey and a towel in my mouth to keep me down under his knife. It wasn't fun, but it was easier than usual.

It took an hour before it was over, and I finally opened my eyes to watch the doc make himself a fix while Connie taped my shoulder and upper arm. When he was finished, he sighed and put the syringe away before tossing a tiny lead pellet onto the table at my side.

"Twenty-five or twenty-two," he said.

"Twenty-two," I grunted. "A goddamn sparrow killer."

"One of the fair sex, no doubt." Mattlocks grinned. "It would have done the job with that vein cut though. The trouble with the small ones is that you can talk yourself into thinking they won't kill you, and die on your feet." He paused. "Business usually picks up with you back in town, Jericho."

I ignored the remark and said, "One of my old girl friends was unhappy."

"You wouldn't know why, I suppose?"

"I'm trying to figure that one out," I said, and took out my wallet. "I either got used for a target for what I had done, or for what someone is thinking I'm going to do. It could be she just didn't like me anymore too."

"Give yourself a few days to figure it out," he said. "Don't tear that stitching loose." He watched me. "That is if you've got a few days left in town."

I paid him, and kept my good arm around Connie as we left. I needed more than the rest Mattlocks had suggested. I needed information and some pieces to fit together in the Candoli mess. It was beginning to look like everyone had decided that I was on the other side. And though Judy might have had enough personal reasons to pull the trigger, she might also have been doing a favor for her shack-up. That sort of thinking gave me one more place to worry about a slug coming from, and it made me wonder who Judy's shack-up was, because she had seemed very sure that I would upset her plans for future mink coats by being around. It was another question to have T-Bone work on while I healed up a bit. I wasn't eager to greet the next old friend and get a slug for a hello—I didn't need any more surprises like that.

"Sorry to drag you into this, Connie," I said when we were back in the car.

She shook her head. "I've seen worse. That Vann bitch

must really hate you. She must really be something too, getting you to come back for seconds after five years. Did you think she had changed any?"

"I didn't think she'd shoot me," I said, and frowned at her. "You've been doing your homework, haven't you? How in hell do you know it was Judy?"

She smiled. "So I'm nosy. You came home with a half-ass job of bandaging on you, and I had to convince the sidewalk crowd that you were drunk. Don't you remember telling me to get Gonzales on the phone to find Mattlocks?"

I shook my head. "I didn't realize I was that far gone." I thought for a moment. "I guess I did lose a lot of blood. Did Speedy tell you about Judy?"

"He told me where you had gone from there. And I guess everyone knows that a small gun is a woman's weapon." Her eyes took on a blank look. "Your little blond playmate is your own business. I just thought she'd done it."

"Forget about her now," I told her, and settled back against the seat feeling a warm sense of relaxation from Mattlocks' pain killer. I was glad he'd added a few extra tablets for the next few days.

I lighted a cigarette, and watched Connie irritably jump a red light at the next corner. "She's still a bitch in my book."

I grinned, and smoked silently for a while, so relaxed I could think about the stink the contract had without any past ghosts loose in my mind. There was still no form or pattern to the past few days. I'd run into Greek, Decker, Otto, Jo-Jo, and Judy, and I hadn't gotten one damn thing but trouble and lies from any of them.

Maybe the city had more heat than I thought, and I was pushing too hard; but I couldn't see Bicek as being able to have that sort of control. Still, I was five years rusty, and maybe I couldn't see where the heat was. I knew I'd have to reschedule my plans and dig up a few facts before I did any more pushing. It seemed like a good idea to know who was willing to put holes in me, since I already had more than I needed. T-Bone could get me some helpful information maybe, and since Mattlocks had said rest, I wasn't going to mind staying off the street.

Connie had been silent for a long time, and kept her eyes on the traffic when I glanced at her. "What's with you, redhead?"

She chewed at her lip, and didn't turn her head. Then she shrugged, wet her lips, and asked, "Did anything happen to her? You didn't . . . ?"

"One thing I don't do is take a chance of more prison unless it's over a job. I'm not sure Judy is connected to the job yet. But why don't you lay off the subject? The way I call it right now is that Judy tried to save a good thing for herself, one that she thought I'd mess up. Maybe I will when I find out what it is. Right now she's unhappy as hell, but she isn't dead. I want the people behind her popgun play, if there are any."

Connie glanced at my face, but said nothing. I watched her study the traffic silently for a few blocks before she said, "All right. What happens now?"

"You heard what Mattlocks said." I grinned. "I guess the apartment won't kill me for a few days. You can prove your domestic talents while I use up Mattlocks' pain killer and do some thinking."

She offered me a thin smile. "You can test out my cooking too."

I closed my eyes and thought about when Judy had started showing interest in our apartment's kitchen. Then I said, "You clean house, do the laundry, and cook; what else do you do, Connie?"

"I sell my ass," she snapped. "Is that the answer you want? Why in hell can't you just let things alone?"

"Okay, we'll let them ride," I said. "What you do is your business. If you want to do the domestic bit, fine. I can't kick on that. If you want to start a hustle right away, that's fine too."

"I'll play the domestic bit," she said quietly.

I opened my eyes and studied her face, waiting a long moment before I said, "Look; you're okay, redhead. Thanks for being there."

She hesitated a moment, then shrugged and smiled. "It took you a lot to say that, didn't it? I wasn't asking for anything else, Jericho."

Even with the slugs and the past few days, I relaxed and thought some about Connie. You run into a certain type of girl on the edge of Syndicate and racket business wherever you go. They all wear the same expression, the marks, and the look in their eyes, while they keep on trying. What they work at is a trial run at compatibility. They find someone and they give what they have, before they glance off and go on to the next one, until there is someone who fits. It gives them a lot of memories of apartments like the one Connie and I had, and of motels.

Like a fussy shopper who gets paid to try on a lot of shoes on the off-chance that one pair will fit. And the time in between is a lonely transition period of many beds. Any thought of undying romance is a vague illusion that they won't quite give up, but they will settle for security with a bit of companionship.

I knew Connie was looking, like most of us were, only she had a lot of years full of disillusion yet before she reached the point of giving up. I had reached the point where I was sure my way of life was not compatible to anything but the rackets. Being the Judas wasn't a tag that you could resign from. But even so, I couldn't shake that something in the back of my mind that made me keep on looking. I just put it in second place; the looking to be done after the next contract.

I didn't know what Connie had decided to do about her looking. I've known a few of the young ones like her over the years, and I've never pitied them, because they understand. It's not all fun, and not all of them make it. In fact, only a damn few make it, and the rest go on to a life of alcoholic dreams someplace with a young oldness in their eyes, and dreams to share their loneliness. But a few get out to the mortgaged house and runny-nosed kids, and it's enough for them. So the odds are about standard in life all the way around. Only a few make it at anything.

I found myself hoping that Connie would be one of those who did make it after the thoughts of true love vanished, and romance became a vague state of seldom-sought fantasy. I like the girls like Connie, because in a way they are the strong ones who use what they have to get what they hope for. The lucky ones realize too that their dreams are simply a welcome escape from reality while they wait.

I shook off the thoughts, and glanced at Connie beside me, before I started to concentrate on the present problems again. I needed a rest, and could take it with T-Bone out and looking for some of the answers I needed about Otto and Jo-Jo and the others. Maybe a few days would give the local talent time to move again, before I went to Anna Ryan or started looking for Lora Franks and other goodies like Bicek and Candoli. It might even give Bicek a chance to make a mistake and begin to think that maybe I wasn't going to pay him a social call.

I spent the next day in bed, kicking the thoughts of the contract around, and I put T-Bone on the things I wanted to know. On July 27, a long, hot Sunday, I grew restless, and let Connie drag me out on a tour of the town. It was a day filled with relaxation for her, and an uneasy feeling for me, because I couldn't understand her happiness when being out of my environment made me feel spooky. I realized during those days that she wouldn't ask me what I was there for, and I thought a lot about the chance that I could start enjoying her company too much.

And on Monday morning I knew it was over. I woke up and watched her sleeping face, telling myself that I was looking at a whore who I had let make me dream because I hadn't lived with a woman for five years, and I didn't need to dream or to doubt my vocation. I brought back my own reality by thinking, and the thoughts came like the sun through the window that began to cut into my eyes with its glare.

Figuring that Anna Ryan would be the least likely to

be on either side of the fence, I decided that she was the place to start again. I had to find Lora Franks, and learn who Judy was playing house with. Mostly I had to find Lora, who seemed to have been Candoli's private stock after Maria's killing. And Anna would know things like that; she ran a whorehouse, and kept track of what could be useful talent around town.

As I dressed Monday morning Connie said that it was too soon to go out in the city, but she didn't ask where I was going. She wanted another day or a few more days of the sun and fun that had started on Mattlocks' advice. I couldn't blame her for that, because five years in the pen had made the last few days too good for me too. They had made me think that being out of the gutter, and the stink, and the problems I lived with was a good idea, and I knew it was time to get back to the death and distrust I made my living at. I managed to remind myself of that while I dressed and shaved.

Connie busied herself around the kitchen, until I came out of the bedroom and picked up my hat. "If I get a call from a guy named T-Bone, tell him I'll call him back as soon as I get a chance."

"All right," she said, and waited.

I smiled at her. "What I'm going to do is visit a whorehouse this morning. At least I'm going to visit the owner."

"An old and dear friend, no doubt."

"Yes. A friend. You should meet her someday." I watched her, and considered. Finally I added, "Look, kid, when all this is over, you'll likely go back to playing the call girl or free-lance bit; and uptown or not, that's a one-way road. You'll get a vice squad bust and a record sooner or later."

She watched me and waited.

"Anna's an old friend of mine," I went on. "I think she'd take you into her place if I asked. It sure as hell would beat working for a creep like Decker. Anna runs a clean house, she's fair with her girls, and her trade is willing to pay a hundred an evening easy."

"Thanks for the recommendation," she said quietly. "I should get a letter from you describing my talents when you leave, I guess."

"Oh, for Christ's sake," I said. "I hope the rest of the day isn't like it's starting out to be." I paused for a moment. "What have you got planned for the day?"

She stared at me blankly, then smiled tightly. "I think I'll go downtown and turn a few tricks—just to keep in practice."

I pulled on my hat and headed for the door. "Sure," I said. "You do that." I grinned at her from the doorway. "Have fun, redhead, and remember, try to get paid first, huh?"

She was reaching for an ashtray to throw as I eased out the door.

Anna Ryan's place is what I said. She ran what was known in the city as a snob-hill sort of whorehouse. But whatever you called it, there was never any doubt around town, or with the vice squad cops who took their payoff from her, that she ran a clean house. You didn't get VD or rolled at her place, and she didn't sucker in any girls who didn't know their business. She also didn't get raided, because her clients were people who might embarrass the arresting officers. A girl had to have looks and experience before she went to work for Anna. Hers was also what you could call a straight house, and the special-kicks boys weren't welcome.

It was hot again in the city as I drove, and it didn't take long to learn that the short rest I'd taken hadn't improved the ache in my arm. I had a sore, empty sickness in me as I drove.

At ten o'clock I was on the corner of Cleveland Avenue and Thirty-ninth Street, and I pulled the car over and parked in front of the large Old South-type house that Anna called home. It was well kept, with a manicured lawn and fresh paint that helped me remember Anna believed the price of a hundred plus tips entitled a man to some good booze, comfortable conditions, and a willing woman. She didn't lose many customers, thinking like that.

A maid let me in and told me that Anna was in bed with breakfast. Leading me to a curtained sitting room she vanished toward the back of the house with my name. It was cool in the room, and a faint mixture of perfume hung in the air. The warm, musky smell of Anna's own perfume was present, and I remembered how it fit her dark-eyed mixture of Mexican and Irish blood, which made her a lot of woman with a temper tossed in.

The maid returned and led me to a back bedroom and Anna's voice.

"Well, come on in, Jericho," she said from the pillow-piled bed. "I've been expecting you; though it sure takes you a long time to get around to a visit."

"I couldn't get away from my state vacation, Anna." I grinned at her. She hadn't put on her makeup yet, and she looked old and tired, with wrinkles marking her neck and eyes. She had gained some weight and given up the battle with the gray in her black hair, now silver blue with drugstore help.

"Okay," she said, watching my face. "So I look like hell before I get up. You don't have a Florida tan yourself." She pointed to a chair beside the bed, and held out her hand. "Now that you've gotten half the town talking about you, I suppose you need a place to cool off at." She shook her head. "You'll never change, you bastard. The years took some of the wild out of you though—it shows."

I pulled up the chair. "So I look like hell too before breakfast," I said grinning. "But I'm not looking for a place to lay up, Anna. I'm looking for a talk."

She sobered, and the smile faded from her face as she sipped at her coffee. "Jericho," she asked, "do you have to be all business all of the time?" She winked. "Here I provide a service for men night after night for the past twenty years, all business, and I sleep alone. The one remaining thing that has any pleasure is seeing old friends—and even they come to me on business. I'm going to get a complex." She swept the bed covers aside and stared at me. "Would you like to go to bed with me?" she asked bluntly. "It would give my girls something to think about."

I grinned. "Have I ever tried to take you to bed, Anna?"

"There you are," she sighed. "Men come to me on business, and take my girls to bed. I'm beginning to think that the hardest thing in the world is for an owner of a cat house to get laid. So my enjoyment in life is old friends and gossip, but you vanish for five years and come back to make even that business. I wish I *was* thirty years younger, so I could take you to bed." She studied my face. "You're back here on a job, aren't you?"

"An important one, Anna," I said. "Or I'd take you out to a nice long dinner and ease the news out of you a little bit at a time."

"You would too." She smiled. "Take me out to dinner and then come back here to sleep with one of the girls. How old do you think I am, Jericho?"

I studied her blandly. "About seventy," I ventured.

She laughed. "Same old bastard, aren't you?" she said. "I'm only fifty-two. Come around once looking for experience, and I'll give it to you." She took a deep breath and patted the front of her nightgown. "Do those look like seventy? I could still show you a few things."

"You always could, Anna," I said. "Only right now I want you to *tell* me a few things."

She sighed. "All right, business then. I'm an old beat-up tramp, and I'll cry in my coffee while you ask me questions about Blacky Shaw and Judy. I don't know what else you're after, but it will help my image to have the girls know I've got a man in my room. What can I do for you?"

"How did you know what I wanted?"

"Honey, customers talk a lot in bed, the girls pass things on to me, and I've got nothing to do but add things up."

"Can you add up anything that got Blacky killed? Any

trouble with Bicek or that bunch—hell, anything at all?"

"That's crazy," she said. "Blacky didn't want any part of that. He came around when he had an extra hundred as usual, but no trouble." She stopped, her face thoughtful. "Well, there was some trouble here one night, but—no, he was just drunk."

"What do you mean?"

"It was the night he got killed. He came in here drunk, and asked for one of the girls who was already busy. Honestly, Jericho, in his condition he could have screwed an open window and never known the difference. But he wanted her, and just stamped out in a huff when she wasn't available. Like she was the only ass here."

"Who was it? The girl?"

"Pearl, I think," she said. "He didn't really have any favorite here. I don't usually remember things like that. You know how Blacky was. But it was what he said that made me remember. He said he was getting tired of second choice and getting pushed around in this town, and he knew something that was going to get him the best of everything from now on." She paused, and wondered about that. "You think he really did know something?"

"Yeah," I said. "I think he knew enough to get himself killed."

I took the picture of Candoli from my pocket and handed it to her. "Seen him around, Anna?"

"One of Iron Mike's men," she said without looking up. "Mike brought him here once, I suppose to show him around the city's hot spots." She sighed. "No big news, that one. I haven't seen him since." She picked up her coffee cup and emptied it. "Now I suppose you want to talk about Judy. I always told you she was a bitch. If you wanted that kind as a playmate, I could have sent you a girl to keep house. At least then you wouldn't have done five years in the pen for handing out what some bastard deserved."

"The cops didn't look at it quite like that."

"All I'm saying is that if she had been one of my girls she would have had sense enough not to use your bed. What do you want to know about little Judy anyway?"

"Who's she shacking up with now?" I asked, feeling the dull ache in my shoulder. "And I'm not set on rehashing a dead issue. I hear she's not hooking anymore."

"Whoring, you mean," Anna said. "Some women are whores by profession, and some by nature. Judy isn't ever going to stop being one by nature, and for you she couldn't be hard to find; she'll be right where she can gain the most with that body of hers."

"Whose side was she on during the takeover?"

"She'll be on the winning side, and with as big a man as she can get next to. But I don't know whose bed she puts her shoes under nights." She shook her head. "Why don't you stay out of that stupid war, and I'll give you a job here."

"I'd kill myself in a week." I grinned at her. "Just the fringe benefits."

"Better that way than going with a hole in your head."

I slumped back in the chair and rubbed my eyes, remembering Speedy's description of Lora Franks.

"Let's try another girl, Anna. Lora Franks. Small and

dark, a damn good-looking kid with a lot of breast and hip. She needed everything she had to be a stripper at the Blackstone. Sixteen or seventeen years old, I hear."

"Picking them sort of young, aren't you, Jericho?" Anna lighted a cigarette and nodded. "I know the one you mean. One show a night under the hot lights and the rest of the night under hot sheets." She smiled. "Belonged to the Perille bunch."

"Any idea where she is now?"

A glimmer of interest crossed Anna's face. "A whorehouse is the greatest place in the world for news on people. The word is out that little Lora Franks went the route during the takeover, and wound up on the bottom." She shrugged her shoulders and went on. "It seems that she was doing some other shooting too before it was over —heroin, I think. One of that bunch put her on it, and she went from the top to the bottom—right down to some five-dollar cat house. I don't know where; just look for the one with the longest line. Does that help any?"

I smiled. "I don't know where it fits yet, but Lora seems to be my only lead to Candoli."

"That's your job in town then, finding Candoli?" she asked. "It's a good way to get killed."

"I needed a buck. I took an easy job."

"And you would have starved without it, huh?" she asked. "What will you say on the next one, or the one after that? You seem to be in a hurry to find a coffin."

"It's a living."

Anna nodded, then smiled. "Pity is a bunch of shit, Jericho. So I don't pity you a bit for being hooked on that gun like some men get hooked on cards or booze. I've just known you too damn long to even like the idea that you're in a business you can't win at. You'll know too much about things someday, and the contract will have your name on it. What then?"

"Then I'll come around and take that job as bouncer."

She shook her head and smiled. "Come back when you're not working," she said. "I'll treat you to a free night around here."

I picked up my hat and winked. "I wonder if Lora Franks will do the same when I find her."

eight

I drove back to Ninth Street in the close heat after I left Anna's, and had little doubt in my mind that whatever had happened since I'd started looking for Candoli was tied into Bicek and Iron Mike. Like Blacky's getting shot was tied in. But being sure of that didn't help my uneasy feeling about the smell of the job. It stank like an overripe stockyard, because the few things I had learned were too indefinite to account for an effective takeover of the empire Perille had run. It was amateurish on both sides, from blowing Noto's brains out to the shooting of

Black Maria. I didn't add it up to a takeover; I added it up to suicide for Bicek.

But Bicek was very much alive and Mike wasn't. So it also stank like a job you can get killed at shouldn't stink, and I already had two holes in me for learning that bit of wisdom. My shoulder ached with the thought, and I told myself that if that was the going rate for getting wisdom, I wouldn't be around much longer.

Five years had changed the rules a bit. But you still needed a program card to know which snake to shoot first, and I was ready to shoot some. I would, in fact, like nothing better than to have a good solid reason for looking up Bicek and sending him on the same ride Blacky had taken.

That was all I needed—one reason—and my shoulder came close to being reason enough. I could feel the ugliness growing inside me along with an uneasy feeling that I was being snickered at by someone who was not paying my bills.

I cruised the old neighborhood, and thought about Lora Franks, as I wondered where to start this time. I just had the name of a hooker to go by, and a lot of heat, and no one I could trust enough to start asking questions of—at least I couldn't start asking questions about Lora among my pretty shaky list of past friends. So I had a certain amount of heat, plus the name of a well-stacked little dish who whored and shot heroin and who might be my only remaining clue to Bicek and Candoli. She should know why Candoli had vanished, just as she had. I still thought the river was a good choice for Candoli—

a short swim with a junkyard tied to his legs.

Deciding that I needed a drink, I headed for Greek's. I needed a drink because I was mad, and I hurt, and I couldn't think straight anymore. I wasn't a damn detective who had all the time in the world to sit around and figure out the pros and cons of some amateurish power grab that shouldn't have worked in the first place. I was about ready to take the contract money back to Candoli and say, "I think we had better quit while we're ahead on this, old man, and you can go on with your dying, because you're not going to like what I'll find, and I'm not going to like what I'll do when I find it."

I called myself a stupid bastard, and I went to Greek's for that drink and to start all over again.

Greek was happy to see me, and to take a ten for the little he knew about Lora, which was about the same as Speedy and Anna had told me. I worked my way through my second drink while I used Greek's phone to call the Blackstone and then T-Bone; I drew a blank at both places. Lora, it seemed, was not in the habit of making it easy for people to find her.

I thought about that while I watched Greek and wondered how long it would take him to get to a phone after I walked out. He'd put the word out now, and once it was known that I was looking for Lora, they would start looking too, or they would simply try to stop me from finding anything.

That was fine if you liked making yourself a target.

I finished my drink and went back into the heat again, to try to make some sense out of what was going on, while I set myself up as the bait. I had Candoli's picture in my pocket, and Lora as the question to ask in the bars and hotels on Ninth.

I started with the strip joint next to Greek's, and worked my way down the street. The bartenders and desk clerks were not happy with my questions. They eyed Candoli's picture, and the bulge of the .45 under my jacket, and quickly told me that they knew nothing, and they likely hoped like hell I'd go off and get myself shot at some competitive establishment. People are not very cordial when a man begins to ask loaded questions that are bound to make him highly unpopular with the local talent.

I covered the street, and took my time at it, until there were no more dives to work, and the evening was coming alive around me with neon. I stopped at a bar and spent some more time over some whiskey before I visited the can and checked the clip in the .45, then I went back to Greek's to see what sort of results my day of being nosy had gotten.

With a guy like Greek you can tell how much heat you've generated with the wrong people by the way he'll look scared and shy away from you. One look at Greek, and I knew I was hot. I knew too that I wouldn't win the best-liked-man-in-town prize.

Greek saw me easing onto a bar stool and started for the far end of the bar to work down there. He would have made it too, except I caught his eye and waved him over.

"Hello, Greek," I said, and watched the corner of his mouth twitch while a fast fake smile slid over his face.

He lighted a nervous cigarette that he didn't need, stared at it with distaste for a moment before putting it out, then said, "Look, Jericho, if you want to get yourself knocked off, don't drag me into it."

"I just like your company, Greek."

His lips started to twitch again and he glanced at the door. "Man, you're bad news to be seen with right now."

"Who says?"

"Half the town, damn it! You've leaned on everybody on this street today, man. And you sure as hell weren't quiet about it."

"Hell, I thought all I was doing was asking a few simple questions."

"Simple to you, sure. You're nuts, man! You got to keep pushing Bicek until he ain't got a choice but to put a DOA tag on your toe. You can get bumped for being just nosy."

I smiled at him. It was the way I had to start now. I wanted someone to know that I was going to be a severe pain in the ass until I had an answer, or until they sent someone around to stop me from looking. It's not a fun thing to play at when you know that a slug in the guts, and a swim in the river, are the things you can expect for asking too many questions. But there is one advantage in setting yourself up as a target—you know that the ones who come after you will have some of the answers you want.

All you need to do is stay alive and ask the questions.

Greek looked at me like I was already dead and my coming back and bringing my questions with me didn't make him happy. The fear that showed deep in his eyes kept him sweating and looking at the night outside like he was expecting someone.

"I told you everything I know, Jericho," he said. "I don't know anything about Blacky or any of that. Why do you keep it up?"

"Blacky's dead," I said.

"Yeah. So that's Blacky. Me, I don't want to get the same way. Leave me out, Jericho."

"Greek"—I smiled—"Blacky wasn't killed for the lousy few bucks he had in his wallet that night. It was still there when the cops found him."

"I don't care what he was killed for. I don't want any bullets in my head like Noto."

"Look, you simple bastard. Blacky got killed for knowing too much, and he didn't learn what got him killed at Decker's or Anna's."

"What do you mean?"

I kept my smile. "Blacky was killed for something he saw here that night. He learned something that it wasn't safe for him to know. What makes you think that someone isn't going to start thinking that you know the same thing?"

"No," Greek said. "Nothing happened here that night."

"I hope nothing did, Greek," I said. "I wouldn't like to find out that you'd been lying to me."

Greek tried to smile, while he sweated and looked away from me quickly. I wondered how it was to live in his kind of fear—the kind that kept his eyes veiled with a nameless waiting, while they searched and shifted around like running black bugs each time the door opened. I hoped that I had added enough new fear to what was already there to cause him a lot more sleepless nights, because his face told me that my guess about the reason for Blacky's death was something he knew, or had seen that night.

I told Greek that I'd be back, and left him to remember and worry about what he'd done as I went outside into the night again. I stood on the sidewalk and took my time lighting a cigarette, while I looked toward my rented car where it was parked a half block away. There didn't seem to be anything unusual happening to break the pattern of the evening, and it made me wonder if I hadn't wasted a day making myself unpopular.

I was about halfway to the car when I got the first hint that someone else was unhappy with my day's activities. Even in city traffic there's a pattern when you're looking for a change in it, and I caught the sudden sound of a car being started, and saw the lights of the car parked at the next corner go on, as it pulled out into the light traffic. It was timed nicely to allow me to get to the traffic side of my own car, and have my back to the street when they reached there. My stomach grew tight as I kept walking.

I made my way down the sidewalk with a slight stagger, like a man would if he'd been making the bars all day, and that's exactly what they expected; I'd been making the bars and running my mouth. I could feel a coldness creep slowly into my brain as I caught the dull glint of gun metal near the open back window of the oncoming car.

Whoever my friends in the car were, they were using

one of the oldest wiping procedures in the books, but one that when handled by pros was as deadly as a close-quarters ambush. I could vouch for the procedure, because I'd used it myself, and I also knew its flaws. The timing was the thing. Ideally their car should arrive beside mine at the same time I turned my back to the traffic and opened my door. There was little chance of missing a man's back at the eight-foot range there should be between the two cars then.

The speed of the approaching car held steady as I walked, and I hoped earnestly that the two in the car were pros. It would make the flaw in the procedure easier to take advantage of. I gauged the distance to my car, as I knew they were doing, and watched them pick up speed. I'd learned the timing lesson involved in this kind of hit the hard way, and I knew how easy it was for a pro to be oversure of himself.

I didn't like the fact that it appeared I wouldn't get a chance to talk to whoever I suckered in with my nosy act, but it wasn't time to freeze or to back off. It was time to move and keep moving. I blew their timing by moving too soon, stepping off the curb three cars in front of my own and going down on the hot asphalt with the .45 in my hand. I could hear the squeal of tires as they picked up speed, and I rolled under the front of the parked car, peering out in time to get a brief glimpse of Otto, as he fought to correct the mistake and pushed the sawed-off shotgun out the window so he could shoot down at the street from the speeding car.

Buckshot, I thought. And then there was no more time for thinking because the car was going past, and the twin bores of the twelve-gauge were coming down.

Watching Otto's face edge in panic as though the scene was being played in slow motion, I put three slugs through the door he was leaning on, because I knew that it wouldn't stop the .45 slugs at that range. I saw him jerk with the impact of the first two slugs as they slapped into him, and there was no doubt about the third slug, which plowed a bare metal gulley over the edge of the window and glanced up to bloom on Otto's throat like a red poppy. Otto's sawed-off roared and drowned out the growl of the .45, and everything blended into the crash of breaking glass behind me and the squeal of tires on hot asphalt as their car lurched past. I put two more slugs through the back of the car, aiming where Jo-Jo should be sitting, and watched with satisfaction as the car lurched, sideswiped a parked car, and climbed the curb with a scream of tortured steel, coming to rest in a storefront. I counted three shots, figured seven yet in the clip, and stayed where I was, thumbing the hammer back as I waited for Jo-Jo. I was going to put two hundred grains of lead right where they would do the most good if he came out—I happen to resent getting shot at.

It had taken less than a minute for the shotgun attempt, or you could say it had taken a lifetime—Otto's lifetime. I enjoyed the solid feel of a .45 bucking in my hand again, and knew that the bait had paid off. Otto's and Jo-Jo-s interest in Lora Franks was either to shut her up or to make sure I didn't find her. It helped to make me realize how important she was to find.

The street was silent except for the far-off growing

wail of a police car, but I could feel the curious eyes on me from behind the windows on Ninth. They were eyes I didn't need to worry about, I knew, because cops were the enemy to them.

Keeping one ear on the police sirens, I watched the car in the storefront with the hope I could give Jo-Jo a slug in the guts. If Jo-Jo was conscious in the car, he would be hearing the sirens too, and know that time was running out for him to move.

He came out of the car in a staggering run, looking all the world like a drunk with the shit cramps, and with no gun showing. I leveled the .45, and led him a little to allow for his run, then hesitated. Holding his gut, he ran toward me on the other side of the street. I started to squeeze a round off that would have sent him to the promised land, but as I listened to the sirens, very close now, he turned into an alley across the street and vanished. I thumbed the hammer forward on the .45 and watched the black void a moment to make sure he wasn't coming back out, then I hurried toward the river on Ninth and cut into the next cross alley. Jo-Jo had made his second mistake for the night, I knew. The one that would be fatal. He had gone into the short end of an L-shaped alley, which would soon have the cops plugging up the place where he had entered and just me, the dark, and the rats between himself and his going-away place.

I didn't think he had quite figured on that when he made his choice. That's one of the advantages of knowing the city as I did, I decided, as I picked my way through the rubble. At least for this stage of the game I had the winning hand, and soon I'd have a warm body to answer some questions for me. I wanted to know why my being dead was worth outside talent, to start with; and I might play with him a bit, simply because I didn't like getting shot-gunned.

I paused in the dark to listen to the familiar sounds, muted, of Ninth Street behind me, and felt the slipperiness of the alley under my feet. Brushing waves of disturbed flies from my face, I tried to think of other things besides the smell around me. But I smiled through every minute of it, until I reached the place I wanted, and stood waiting in the dead dark with the foraging rats to keep me company.

I heard Jo-Jo coming long before I saw the darkness of his body moving in the shadows. He stumbled and cursed in a voice that was wire-edged with fear and pain, and he fell into the slime twice before he was close enough for me to hear his heavy breathing.

He was taking deep gulps of air and fighting the panic of being trapped in the dark when he paused in front of me, and I stepped softly across the two yards that separated us. I pressed the cold nose of my .45 into the soft flesh under his ear, saying, "Let's talk, Jo-Jo," and I let him listen to the double click of the .45's hammer going back.

It must have sounded like death to Jo-Jo. "Judas," he said, like he was praying. He remained motionless a moment, except for the heaving of his chest. Then he coughed and sat down hard in the rubbish, grunting in a babbling, choking way.

I kept the .45 pressed against his neck and searched him quickly for a gun before I squatted down in front of him. He jerked in pain as my hand went over his chest, and his face twisted into a bleak smile I could see vaguely in the dark.

"Smashed up inside," he said. "You're a lucky bastard, Judas."

I nudged him in the chest with the muzzle of the .45, and heard him gasp. "Who sent you, Jo-Jo?" I asked. "Did Bicek waste good money on a couple of flops like you and your partner?"

Jo-Jo worked at it, then he laughed softly. "Still shooting in the dark, ain't you? You'll never find out, Judas. There's a lot of things you'll never find out."

"Like what?"

"Things you wouldn't understand," he said. "It's too bad you had to pick a loser this time."

"For you it's a loser." I kept smiling and nudged him again where it hurt. "Shooting in the dark got me you, didn't it?"

His body sagged toward me. "It got you nothing."

"Maybe Lora Franks will take care of that when I find her," I said, grinning. His head was drooping, and I slapped him suddenly. "Jo-Jo," I told him, "you're going to hurt a hell of a lot more than you do now if we don't have a nice friendly chat."

He simply kept leaning forward, pressing against my gun, and then silently fell over on his side into the slime. I rolled him over and held a match over his eyes. I didn't have all night to play with Jo-Jo after all. He'd gotten around to making his last mistake.

I looked at the body a moment, then sighed and dropped the pistol back into my coat pocket. It had cost someone Otto and Jo-Jo to prove they didn't want me finding Lora or Candoli. I hoped it was worth it.

I was tired of the stink in the alley, and began to walk, leaving Jo-Jo to the rats after I had wiped his .45 clean with my handkerchief and eased it into his pocket. And all at once I was tired of looking for ghosts and whores in the anonymity of the city. There was a sudden thought of Connie when I left the alley and headed casually toward the car.

I was opening the door when the police car idled to a stop beside me, and a gruff voice ordered, "Just keep your hands on the door, Jones."

"What is this?"

"This is keep-goddamn-still-and-don't-do-anything-stupid time," the cop said. "We got a pickup on you."

"On what charge?"

The second cop came around the back of the car and shook me down. Then he snapped the cuffs on my wrists, saying, "If you don't know, then you're in good shape." He grinned.

"What the hell?" I asked. "Haven't you guys got enough to do without making phony pinches?"

"Oh, we've had a very busy night," the cop said. "So busy, in fact, that Detective Ferris of Homicide just couldn't wait to talk to you when we found out who had rented this car." He held my arm and motioned toward the prowl car. "You can save the innocent act of bewilderment for Ferris, pal. He's eager to hear your sad tale."

I shrugged and got into the car. It looked like it was going to be one of those nights.

At headquarters, the building as well as the routine hadn't changed. I'd made the "pick and hold" lineup enough times to know the procedure better than a rookie. I knew the routine well enough to start wondering what was up when my escorts led me past the interrogation rooms and the check-in desk, and headed down the winding corridor to the office at the end.

The patrolmen took the cuffs off me and pointed toward the door. "Inside, Jones. They're expecting you."

I read the gilt letters on the door and shrugged as I went inside. It was a large room with paneled walls and thick carpets. One wall was covered by a bookcase filled with files and well-used binders of court cases. The cluttered desk seemed massive by contrast to the small man seated behind it. Ferris stood leaning against the bookcase, staring absently at me.

I grinned at him. "If I'd known you wanted a social call, Ferris, I'd have dropped in without an escort." I stared at the man behind the desk. "Or did our famed DA, Mr. Turner, set up this little chat?"

Turner nodded at the chair in front of his desk and folded his hands across his chest. He was thin, with dark hair, and a perpetual scowl to match his cold eyes. "Sit down, Jones," he said. "I thought it was about time we met."

"Oh, we've met, Turner," I said. "About five years ago, when you hung a five-year rap on me; or had you forgotten?"

"You were guilty," Turner said.

"I did my time too," I reminded him. "Now what in hell is this party about? I don't care to have my nights spoiled by rides in prowl cars."

Turner smiled. "And I don't like my district being used as a shooting gallery."

I dropped into the nearest chair and lighted a cigarette. Then I said, "Well, I guess everyone has his problems. What has your problem got to do with me?"

Ferris stamped angrily to a chair and sat down. "I don't suppose that you know anything about the shooting on Ninth Street this evening, huh?" he asked sarcastically. "So I'll tell you about it."

I listened quietly as he told me about it. Then he added, "You just happened to be parked there, huh? Where were you?"

"Out getting drunk," I said. "Hell, you want me to keep a timetable for you? As far as I'm concerned, they can shoot up the whole street every night! Maybe that's the answer to the population explosion, huh?"

"You don't listen too good," Ferris said. "That shooting tonight was one of the sort that backfired on the shooters."

Turner watched us. "That could mean there will be more shooting," he said. "I wouldn't like that."

"I don't suppose whoever is getting shot at will like it either."

Ferris and Turner talked a moment in a low tone; I couldn't catch their words. Then Turner settled back in his chair and sighed. "Off the record, Jones, just who *is* trying to kill you?"

"Off the record, Turner, go to hell," I said pleasantly.

A flash of anger moved across the DA's face. "Do you deny that there are a couple of guns from Chicago looking for you? Ferris has assured me that he informed you about your Chicago friends, namely Otto and Jo-Jo. Since the man shot tonight was Otto, I think we can lock you up for your own safety and make it stick."

"I don't think you can," I said. "I think that if you

could, I'd be in a cell right now." I glanced at Ferris. "Your stoolie information wouldn't get me a day."

Turner watched me and lighted his pipe, then shrugged. "All right; we realized that we wouldn't get anyplace with you like this. And I doubt if we'll be able to stop these gangland killings that have occurred here this summer. But!—in your case we are going to stop any possibility of more killings."

"If you're so sure someone wants to kill me, I really hope you do stop him," I said, grinning.

Turner grinned back coldly. "You'd be no loss to the city," he said. "But I'm more concerned with avoiding any more killing."

I watched him blankly. "I still don't know any Otto or Jo-Jo."

"You wouldn't, of course," Turner said. "I could also ask you what Vanatta has against you to send his gunmen down here after you."

I studied him calmly, wishing like hell I *did* know.

"You wouldn't know why two of Vanatta's hatchet men would be interested, huh?"

"How in hell can you be so sure that they're after me? I just got out of the pen."

"You must grow unpopular very fast," Turner said. "I frankly don't care how you're mixed up with the Chicago Syndicate." He pointed the stem of his pipe at me. "I've enough problems with the local punks. I'm going to eliminate as many problems as I can. Beginning with you."

I glanced at Ferris, then back at Turner. "Just how do you figure on doing that, Mr. DA?" I asked sarcastically.

The DA worked his pipe around in his hands and let

me wait a long moment before he said, "Jones, people get travel fever before I issue orders that they're to be picked up on sight for questioning. I'll give you three days. If you don't get out by the end of the month, I'll make this town so hot for you that Vanatta will seem like the easy way out."

"Just a little organized police harassment, huh, Turner?"

"I'm a practical man," the DA said. "I don't want you around, Jones. Not alive or dead. Go and be someone else's headache."

"And if I don't?"

"You'll start thinking that you're doing a life sentence in the city jail. Don't make me prove I can do it."

"He means it, Jericho," Ferris said. "Give yourself a break and get on out of the city."

"There's only one problem there," I said as I stood up and walked toward the door.

"What's that?" Ferris wanted to know.

"Vanatta." I smiled. "He might not like it if I were too hard to find."

As I closed the door I realized that Turner had reminded me of a lot of the past week. There wasn't any logical solution to the problem he brought up. And I reminded myself that Vanatta was no joke, even when you didn't know why he wanted you dead. The contract still had the stink of there being some fine print in it that I hadn't read.

nine

The visit to the station and the day's events kept me quiet and brooding as I drove toward the apartment. It built an ugliness inside me, because there was only one way the pieces might fit. Before I reached the apartment, I had part of the answers for Candoli, and I knew who was backing Bicek.

Jo-Jo and Otto were Vanatta men, all right, and that put their hats into the pot. It didn't explain Blacky or where John Candoli was yet, but it was beginning to settle down to knowing who I could expect to be trying to kill me next.

And in three more days the cops would be on my back too. It left a cut-and-dried solution for me—I had to get my business done quickly. Lora Franks was the first one I needed to talk to. And then I'd have to talk with Bicek and Greek about Blacky, a moment-of-truth sort of talk that should tidy up my Kansas City business and let me go back to Candoli with some answers. I might even return Vanatta's favor when I got there.

That's all I had to do in a three-day period to keep the cops off my back, and I knew Turner hadn't been kidding. He could put enough heat on me so I wouldn't be able to work.

I rubbed my face tiredly while I remembered Connie and the fact that there was something else I needed to do. She had done some changing too since that day at Decker's.

Up to now she had seemed content to play at housekeeping around the apartment. For her it was likely the lesser of two evils, when the other choice is going back on the street. And even for a hooker housekeeping is a way to the fantasy land of vine-covered cottages and dirty diapers. More correctly, so long as she was sharing my apartment any dream of marriage was total fantasy. A dream she would have every time she parked her shoes under someone's bed. I hoped that she would get lucky and find a trick who could fit into her fantasy world. But there wasn't any doubt that my next, not so pleasant, project was to remind her of the fact that our mutual bit of housekeeping was fast coming to an end, and that not all the bastards in the world are named Decker.

The thought stayed with me until I got back to the apartment in time to take her out to a late dinner at a place she had told me she'd worked while Decker had her on the street. She did not want to go, and I said, "Fine, I'll go myself," so she came.

The place was a hotel with a bar-and-restaurant combination downstairs. But it was neither the service nor the drinks that made the place attractive to the johns from downtown out on a romance-seeking excursion. It was the place where the pimps took their whores to show off the merchandise. And it was not considered bad manners to ask a woman her price if she was inside the place.

We had spent half an hour in the place before Connie received her first offer. The john was a fat little man who sweated a lot, and looked like a bald Santa Claus. He had small eyes and pouty lips that trembled as he walked over and stood beside Connie at our table.

"You busy, sweetheart?" he asked. "I haven't seen you around for a while."

Connie pulled her arm from under his soft fingers. "Please," she said, watching me.

The fat man looked at me and said, "Oh, sorry. Connie's an old friend. Didn't mean to—"

"No sweat," I said, watching her. "I don't own her, and I don't do her business for her." I smiled at them both. "So any business you two do will have to be between you."

She looked at me like I'd just spit on the table, and I watched everything that had crept into her face during the past days fade until a professional mask remained.

"Then you wouldn't mind . . ." the fat man began.

I showed him my best smile. "I wouldn't want to think that I was the cause of two good friends not getting together. I mean, if she wants to make a buck or two tonight."

I got up then and went to the bar to get a drink. I could feel Connie's eyes follow me away from the table. And I caught the fat man's loud whisper: "That your pimp now, Connie?"

I didn't hear what her answer was. I stood at the bar and watched the bartender work his way down the bar with a damp rag that he used to pick up what loose change there was beside the glasses. I watched him for five minutes, and I gave him a dollar for my drink.

"Keep the change," I told him.

He looked at me painfully. "There ain't any change, mister."

"Keep it anyway," I suggested.

Connie and the fat man were gone when I turned back toward the table. I finished my drink and left the place with nothing to do but drive around the city and let the brooding eat at my mind while I made the bar stops. I kept it up until I had enough whiskey fog in my mind to dull the past; and the only thing that remained was the present, so I bought myself a bootlegged .38 before I gave in and headed for the apartment, feeling a need for sleep before tomorrow.

I began looking for Lora Franks on Tuesday morning. It was the twenty-ninth of July, and hot again, and I no longer cared where I asked my questions or what the police had thought when they found Jo-Jo in the alley. I wanted simply to finish the contract before the police heat made it impossible, and my time ran out with the end of the month. I knew too that Bicek would be more careful now, and that he didn't want me finding Lora Franks before he did.

Thinking about the police, I realized that I had one advantage that Bicek most likely didn't have—cops are good places to get information too. I didn't think Ferris would give me the right time of day after yesterday's events, but he wasn't the one I was thinking of as I drove uptown.

Just as a man who sells information to the cops is an asset to them, it is also obvious that hoods would be willing to pay for similar information, and that having their own ranks of stoolies would help. To be a stoolie for a hood you need a chance to read police reports. The chief file clerk at headquarters was a stoolie for hoods. He could tell you exactly what the police had on you any time you paid him to tell. I had paid him a few times in the past. I called him on the telephone, and offered to pay him again.

Chief Clerk Wilbur Hightower's prices had gone up since the last time I had used him.

"You're getting expensive, Wilbur. You could run a check before for fifty."

"Do you want it for a hundred or not, Jericho?" he asked. "Look at the chances I take."

"I want it," I told him. "Everything you got on Lora Franks; the whole jacket."

"I can't get all that, Jericho."

"Sure you can," I said softly. "Remember how you told me that nobody wonders where the reports are going? Just give it to one of the office cuties; she'll be happy to make you a copy for the vice squad."

"Sure, sure," he said quickly. "It's just a lot of paper you don't need."

"It's a lot of money for what you get for nothing, pal. When can you have it?"

"Tomorrow."

"No good, Wilbur," I said. It was already 10 A.M. according to my watch. I glanced at it and said, "I'll see you at the Brass Rail at five."

"I can't do it in that time," he said. "It just isn't worth the risk I have to take."

I let him wait for a long while. "Wilbur," I asked, "when do you retire from the nice job with all the fringe benefits?"

Wilbur understood that, all right, because he worried a lot about how he made his pocket money. "I'll try to have it for you, Jericho," he said.

I grinned. "You do that, Wilbur," I said, and hung up the phone.

The call left me with a day of unwanted time, which I spent in the bars until Wilbur delivered. Men like Wilbur always deliver, and I was the owner of a police report on Lora Franks' life. There was nothing in it that should have been read, and I found just one item I wanted.

Perhaps the report should never have been printed. It told nothing about the woman, it simply reported why and when she had received the attention of the vice squad. A police file is fact without trimmings, and the facts on Lora took me the better part of two hours to read. When I was finished, I had what I wanted—the address was a whorehouse near the river. It was a long step down from the Blackstone, and I wondered what had caused it. In fact, it was the end of the line for a whore—a two-dollar house for the river's barge hands in the city's black ghetto.

I tore up the report and left it in a trash can, where it belonged. The rest of finding Lora Franks was easy if you could do that sort of flesh buying.

Lora's pimp sold her to me for the night at the price of twenty bucks, and acted glad to get it. She was in her crib-size room in the old frame firetrap she had lived in since Candoli had vanished. I couldn't figure the fast drop in popularity she'd had. Even being hooked on heroin shouldn't have done that much damage to a body that Black Maria had been willing to kill for.

When I stepped into the room and peered about in the weak glow of a shaded forty-watt bulb, I was glad I had brought a bottle. Lora still had the long, smooth legs and high breasts of a stripper, and you didn't expect to find a body like that in a two-dollar house. But you forgot how good that body looked, and you knew why she was there, when you saw her face. I looked, and then looked away, understanding then why she lived for the next few hours of forgetfulness she could find in a shot of heroin. An auto accident might destroy a face as brutally as hers was destroyed, yet there was a completeness to the twisted wreak of scar tissue that suggested deliberate destruction, and her flawless body made the face seem uglier than it was.

She glanced up when I closed the door, and saw me shift my eyes away from her face. She untied the belt that held her robe together, and motioned casually to the basin of water on the dresser. "Wash," she said. "You can turn the lights out when you're finished."

"Want a drink?" I asked, and held the bottle toward her.

She reached for it like an old friend, "God yes," she said.

I sat at the foot of the bed and watched her drink, as I told her that I was just there for a talk. She told me that talking was easier than screwing, and it didn't matter anymore to her. Then she tied the robe closed again, and we sat on the bed with the bottle between us as we talked.

It wasn't exactly fun—not any of it. I brought it all back to her. She shivered in the room's shadows as I brought Black Maria, and Bicek, and John Candoli back into her scared life.

And when I was finished I didn't have any more doubts about what stank in the contract. I wasn't too happy with myself then, and I wasn't sure that I had really wanted to know the answers, as I watched her fingers clutch at the bottle. Her eyes became darting beads of fear in the shadows of her scarred face when I got up to leave.

I found five twenties in my wallet and tossed them onto the bed, searching my mind for something to say.

Finally I shrugged, and said nothing when I walked out. There were no more pieces to fit into the puzzle now. They were all there as they had been all along. But even a guy like the Judas has to reach a saturation point before he can be sure where the stink is coming from.

I was sure now. I had only been locked up too long to catch it before. It seemed I needed a crash course on the new generation since even the double crosses were getting bigger and better. At the car I spent several minutes thinking it out, and wondered what Bicek would have to say about how nicely the puzzle fit.

I doubted if he would say much at all, as I telephoned T-Bone from a drugstore on Seventh Street, "How are you doing with that information I wanted?" I asked.

"Not so hot," he said. "People are careful about talking."

"How about my friend Bicek?" I asked. "Think he'd be reluctant to talk?"

The line was silent for a moment. "Are you sure you want to see him?"

"Yeah. Real sure. Know where I might run into him?"

The line went silent again for a while, then, "It won't be easy, Jericho. But maybe it could be done. You'd better meet me and we'll set it up."

"Just tell me where he's at." I smiled at the phone. "I'll do the rest."

T-Bone laughed. "You're hot, Jericho. We got to get you in the same building first. There were a couple of Chicago boys who had an accident last night, so things haven't gotten easier. And there's still Gus Gogh and Louie Fendora around." He paused for a long time, like he was figuring the odds. "Better meet me at midnight in the Bunny Club on Thirty-fourth. Know where it's at?"

"I'll find it," I told him. "Will Bicek be there?"

T-Bone let his dry laugh scrape over the line before saying, "He'll be close, Judas. Just don't get impatient."

I listened to the click as the line went dead, and hoped that T-Bone didn't use the time between then and midnight to sell me out to the highest bidder. At least I hoped that he didn't get any heavy offers in that time, because Bicek would be very eager now not to see me.

I drove over to a small bar on Thirty-fourth Street and had a late supper of peanuts and whiskey. Then I nursed my drinks and watched reruns on TV while I waited until it was was time to find T-Bone.

The Bunny Club had a good crowd of late drinkers as well as bar girls working the crowds for their drinks percentage and with the hope that they might still pick up a live one at that late hour. I spotted T-Bone seated in a booth and slid in beside him, asking, "What are you drinking, T-Bone?"

He showed me his snags in a humorless laugh. "Anything you want to buy, Jericho." He signaled for a bartender. "Knowing what you're up to made me think that it's a good time to get all I can from you." He grinned up into the bartender's face as he arrived at the booth. "Got a live one here, Chuck. Let's put some whiskey on the table while he gets his wallet out. None of that bar slop either."

"Whiskey and water," I told him.

"Top shelf," T-Bone said, and looked inquiringly at me. "I hope you brought along enough loot to cover my bill too."

"For what you've dug up, I could cover it with a quarter."

T-Bone nodded. "But that's not the point. It's the risks involved in just asking the questions. It's still fifty a day to be asking them. Anyway, I've got Bicek lined up for you."

"Where is he?"

"Across the street. The Skyline Hotel. His pad and office are on the fifth floor front, like Mike's used to be."

"What room?"

"Five forty-two," T-Bone said, and drained half of his drink in a nervous gulp. "But don't figure that you can walk in on him. He's got Gogh watching in the lobby, and Fendora in the pad with him. You can't go in there cold and expect to make it."

I settled back into the booth. "How do I make it then?"

T-Bone smiled, and nodded toward the girl who was seated two booths from us. "That's Babs," he said. "She has a set of empty luggage in her car outside, and reservations at the Skyline for a Mr. and Mrs. Walker. The room she has is four forty, front." He paused a moment. "That gets you in and past Gogh if he don't know you."

"He doesn't," I said. "Any ideas on how to work it once I'm up there?"

T-Bone shook his head. "That's your ball game in there. Babs will help you get in, and you know where Bicek is at." He shrugged and finished his drink. "Those are tough odds when you still have Bicek and Fendora to go against."

I nodded and grinned. "At least I know where they're at," I said. "It could come as a surprise to them." I took out my wallet and counted out T-Bone's fee, then added fifty bucks to it for the girl. "I'll send her away once we get into our room."

T-Bone nodded and eased out of the booth. "Give us five minutes, and she'll be waiting outside." A moment later he added, "She can give you a layout of the place too. For Blacky I hope you make it."

I hoped so too while I sat and waited those five minutes trying to pin down some vague uneasiness. Then I ran out of time, and went outside to get into the waiting car with Babs. She looked like a girl who was tired from a long trip, but maybe the drive we took around the block was a long one for her.

Spotting Bicek's hired gun inside the lobby of the Skyline was no problem at all. In fact, in that décor it would have been like overlooking a dog turd in a teacup. The lobby was large and cool, with thick rugs over tile floors, and the pastel drapes on the windows added just the right touch of color against the pearl gray monk's cloth that covered most of the walls. The usual collection of armchairs and couches in the lobby were of severe black and white leather, and appeared to be comfortable. It was the sort of a setting where you expected to find continental, hand-tailored suits, and well-groomed people. The only reason you would find someone like Gogh there was that the hotel's silent partner had always been Iron Mike's wallet. It seemed that Bicek's wallet was filling the bill at present.

Gogh didn't fit at all in the lobby. He was big-shouldered, and a quick check of the local muscle on the street corner would have singled out his heavy style. The tan fedora he wore was sweat-stained, and the finger-smudged brim was pulled low over his piggish eyes. He wore a black flannel suit that bagged at the knees, and his paste-white shirt had all the stains of his last few meals on it. When Babs asked for our reserved room, the pig eyes that had followed us since we came in drifted back to the paper he was holding. He didn't bother to look up again as we crossed to the elevator. The elevator operator passed us off as a couple of weary travelers, and only stopped chewing his gum long enough to watch Babs' progress down the hall of the fourth floor. I enjoyed the view myself while she led the way to our room.

She dropped her purse on the bed, sat down beside it, and turned to me. "Do you think it went all right?"

"Fine," I said, and crossed the room to the window. "You can pull out of here in about fifteen minutes." I looked out at the street. "Where's the back stairs, Babs?"

"Down the hall to the right. Fire escape is at the end of the center hall."

I grinned at her. "You know the layout here pretty good."

"I should," she said. "I've screwed in every room in this place. When Perille owned it, that is." She smiled at my surprise. "What did you expect, a choir girl?"

I shrugged it off, and glanced at my watch while she opened her large purse and took out a pint of brandy.

"How about a drink? We've got the time, since T-Bone said I should stay at least a half hour."

I went to the bathroom and got the glasses. "T-Bone wants it done right, huh?"

She poured the drinks and tested hers, then she laughed. "I will take him that long to get back to his apartment and put all the chains on the door." She bit at her lip a moment. "Make sure you give me some time after I leave too, all right?"

"All the time you'll need, Babs," I said. "Can you remember anything about Bicek's apartment that will make it easier for me to get in?"

Babs considered the question a moment, then shook her head. "I was in there a few times to get paid by Perille," she said. "It's like this room; just one door. That don't help you any, I guess."

"Oh, you can never tell." I grinned. "I know they aren't going out the back way when I get there, don't I?"

She studied my face, and suddenly decided that she didn't like what she saw there. Then she finished her drink quickly, and decided that she didn't give a damn if T-Bone had enough time to get home and locked up safely or not when the fun started.

I stood at the window, watching her cross the street to the car, before I checked my .38 and started up to the fifth floor with the feeling that the day had gone entirely too good after a bad week. It had gone so well, in fact, that I was beginning to wonder if T-Bone wasn't coppering his bets by setting me up. T-Bone was like that; he would sell me out in a second if he thought I wouldn't be around to resent it in the morning. And he'd made a mistake tonight when he'd asked to get paid before my talk with Bicek. That didn't fit—not when he knew that he could keep adding fifty bucks a day to my bill for his information. I had to be alive for him to collect. His early collection could mean that he didn't expect me to be alive tomorrow.

It could mean too that I'm just the suspicious type.

The thought made me careful when I reached the fifth-floor landing and eased the door open wide enough to look down the hall.

Louie Fendora was standing beside the phone booth in the hall. Right where he could watch the elevators and the stairs, as well as the door to Bicek's apartment.

I didn't think he was waiting for a bus.

ten

I stood on the landing and fought down the impulse to curse the fine art of cross and double cross that winds its way through a kill contract like spiderwebs in an old cellar. The solid togetherness of the underworld is very nearly a total fable. It doesn't exist. The Capos know that, and that knowledge, coupled with fear, binds the elite together until greed weakens the fear.

And I knew that little fact too, because the pull of greed in men is a fault necessary for my business; the hunger for long green is what makes the .38 cylinder spin, and new faces appear while old ones vanish into shallow lime pits.

I *knew* that.

It didn't make me feel any better about my stupidity in giving T-Bone an opportunity to set me up on a sellout. Five years in stir had made me rusty, all right; it had very nearly made me dead. And death is a thin laugh in the background for people like me. I dealt in it, and dealt it out in the spiderweb of double crosses, knowing that I would hear that thin laugh behind my own back someday. And it wouldn't be the Mafia or La Cosa Nostra behind that—not the brotherhood. It would be one little man who had seen too much and talked about it, or one who needed the five-dollar stoolie pay.

I buried my anger at T-Bone in some thinking, and cracked the door open again to view Fendora. He was staring absently at the telephone book, and I decided that it must be very dull reading. At least he appeared tired and bored with his job of waiting.

I considered that for a moment. He evidently expected me to come up on the elevator or stairway and walk casually into the trap, thinking both he and Bicek were in the apartment as T-Bone had told me. And since I didn't know him, he would be just another guest in the hall as I passed, which would give him ample opportunity to put a bullet in my spine, or ass, or wherever he had been told to put a bullet. It was a nice simple plan, and it would have been nice and effective.

I smiled to myself. It would be a shame not to go into the second act of the night's activities after all that planning. I hoped like hell that I was right in my distrustful thinking, as I pushed open the door and started down the hall.

Halfway down the corridor, Fendora glanced up from the telephone book and shoved a cigarette between his lips, making an obvious show of searching his pockets for a light.

He was still looking through his pockets when I started to walk past him, but while his left hand made searching motions, his right hand had settled into the pocket of his jacket. "Have you got a light, buddy?" he asked.

"Sure," I said, and turned quickly. I jerked his jacket open and down, so that it bound him like a straitjacket. He was fighting to get the gun out before it really had time to register with him that I was on to the trap. I used the butt of my own .38 to chop him across the neck, and he sat down next to the telephone with no steam at all left in him.

I helped him get the flat automatic out of his coat then and used it to break his nose and put a lump above his ear, which should have kept him out for an hour or more. In the usual dive I would have left him in the hall —just another drunk sleeping off a load—but in the Skyline's atmosphere I thought better of it, and dragged him down to the linen closet, where I left him wedged behind a pile of dirty sheets. I tested the feel of his gun and thought for a moment about using it on him, because there wasn't any doubt I'd be dead right then if T-Bone hadn't been just a little bit too greedy. Then I shook my head and left him in the closet; killing rats is always more effective when you kill the big ones. Like the one who had put Fendora on my back.

I went down the hall to room 542, with the hope that Bicek was waiting patiently for Fendora to report a dead man to him. I didn't ring any bells, or knock, and I sure as hell wasn't going to say I was the bellboy or such, since he was probably in there waiting for the fun and games to begin in the hall. I tried the knob slowly, and found the door locked, then I stepped back and kicked right at the fancy-looking lock. The sound of wood splintering seemed loud in the quiet hall, and then I was in the room, moving against the wall as I kicked the door shut behind me, and swinging Fendora's automatic to cover the man seated in a large overstuffed chair behind the desk.

"Were you waiting for someone, Bicek?" I asked him.

Bicek froze, halfway out of the chair, while he eyed the gun, and his mouth sagged open. He was a hood who played the role to the hilt, with tailor-made silk suits and diamond cuff links. He even wore the movie version of a hood's sunglasses.

"What the hell is this?" he growled.

"This," I said, grinning, "is a little setup job that backfired. You shouldn't have done that, Bicek. I would have gotten around to you sooner or later. You caused me a lot of trouble, and practically ruined my homecoming. In fact, you spoiled the hell out of it."

He started to sneer, but thought better of it when he looked at my face and the automatic pointed at his belt. "You bought yourself more trouble now," he said. "Who are you?"

"Names don't matter, Bicek. They call me Judas, the

same one you've been having your people shoot at lately. The results are down at the morgue, and there's room for more. You could even say that there's a cold, damp slab waiting for you down there so all your helpers can have company."

His mouth sagged open a little more, and his lips trembled over his carefully capped teeth. "You got the wrong man."

"Bicek," I said softly. "Anything I decide to shoot you for will be deserved. But we're going to take a little ride, so you won't have any doubts."

He said nothing, and moved very slowly to pick up a cigar from the desk, then lighted it.

"We're going over to see Judy Vann, Bicek," I told him.

He began to sweat heavily. "Suppose I say go to hell?"

"Then I'll kill you right here," I said flatly. "And I'll like it. I'll gut-shoot you, and get out like I came in." I shrugged. "Pick your time. I'd just as soon have some questions answered first."

"About what?"

"Minor things. Just small things. You shouldn't have killed Sanitary Blacky, mister."

"I don't know what you're talking about," he said. "I don't even know who the bum was."

"You'll remember," I assured him. "Every lousy mistake you made, you'll remember." I smiled some more. "Now move slow and come around the desk. You get funny, and I'll show you all sorts of tricks that you didn't bother to teach your boys, or are they Vanatta's boys, or maybe . . . ?"

Bicek moved carefully, keeping very still as I lifted

the .45 from his shoulder holster. "Mr. Chief Punk himself, huh?" I asked. "All the show and no guts."

I had him in front of me where I could watch his face, and when I noticed his eyes I remembered the door behind me, and I remembered Gogh, because the eyes were watching something behind me.

I didn't bother to turn around. I knew that if Bicek liked what was back there I wouldn't. Instead I jerked Bicek toward and around me, and shoved Fendora's automatic into his back, as I faced the door and Gogh with Bicek as a shield.

"Go ahead, Gus," I said. "Shoot! Tell him to shoot, Bicek, and if he doesn't get you, I will. I'll live long enough for that."

I could see Gogh's finger tighten on the trigger of the automatic he had pointed at us. "You stupid son-of-a-bitch," Bicek shouted. "Put the gun down."

I kept pushing Bicek ahead of me, and watched the bewilderment give way to panic on Gogh's face. He was remembering Otto and Jo-Jo—and maybe he was wondering where Fendora was. In that bean-size brain of his there was room for just one thing at a time, and he was thinking of death. It might have occurred to him also that I could shoot and he couldn't; and nobody wants to die.

"Shoot, stupid," I said. "Use it or drop it."

Gus Gogh surprised the hell out of me then—he used the automatic. I felt the sudden jerk and shudder in Bicek's body as the bullet ripped through, and the hot burn of a slug whipping past my ribs. The blast of the gun in the room made Gus hesitate a moment, and I used the time to heave Bicek's limp body into him as he shot again. I put all the weight I had behind that shove, and went down with the automatic pointed at Gogh's chest. The panic was still on his face when he saw the bore pointed at his chest, but it vanished when I squeezed the trigger and kept squeezing it.

Gus was a hard man to kill; he was muscle and no brain, and he stood there swaying as the slugs smashed into his chest, until his brain told him he was dead and he leaned past the balance point and crashed to the floor on his face.

I looked at Bicek's dead eyes staring up at the ceiling, and decided that it was too bad that we wouldn't be having that talk with Judy. I turned to Gus then, and smiled a little as I wiped Fendora's automatic clean with my handkerchief. I closed Bicek's hand around it several times before I called it good enough and ran like hell toward the fire escape.

It wasn't exactly the sort of party you wanted to be attending when the cops arrived.

I hadn't gotten to the heart of the rat's nest yet, I knew. But I had enough to go back to Chicago with, and collect the rest of my contract money. Let the rest wait, I decided. Sometimes it's better that way.

In fact, in a few short hours I would have to be out of Kansas City. The DA had given me three days, all right, but that was before he had two new bodies to add to his list. Now I needed some time to let the cops cool off a bit, and time to work out a clear picture of the Perille takeover. At least I needed a clear picture of the part that Tony Candoli wanted to know. I thought I could give him the answers and collect my pay with what I had.

I thought about it as I drove away from the Skyline Hotel, trying to figure out the one mind in the rat's nest that no one was after. I could find the mistakes now. It had taken Lora, and realizing why the power grab had not seemed like it would work but had. And thinking like that, I could guess why Sanitary Blacky had died.

I squinted at the traffic as the details began to fall into place, but a few questions left themselves unanswered. So I needed time for three things: to let the cops cool off, to let some of the heat around the city reach the rat's nest, and to get all the answers. A trip to Chicago would give me that time.

I stopped at a light and looked out at the city without feeling anything. It was always like that. An empty feeling you get when you know you have something you can't wait to get out of you, like a bad taste in your mouth. And beyond that there was the final answer that even the Judas didn't like. An answer that wasn't really part of the contract, but one that needed some attention.

Near the apartment, I asked myself a few why-type questions about Connie, who was one of those people who are brave enough to dream, no matter how much stink is heaped on their lives. And I thought about how it had ended for us.

I arrived at the apartment and, finding it empty, remembered how I had played the pimp last night. Then I called the airport and made reservations. Connie, no doubt, was on the street, picking up her night's wages.

I fixed myself a drink and listened to the empty apartment for a long time. You never know how silent an apartment can be until you hear it like that; with the new dead fresh in your mind and the soon to be dead in your thoughts of tomorrow. An apartment is truly empty then. It creaks and moans with sounds like those of an old man in pain. It is not a place then that you like your own company in.

I found myself a water glass, and took a full fifth of whiskey to bed with me, along with my .38, and neither one of them could match Connie's warmth in bed.

It was late morning when I awoke to the sounds of Connie's dressing. I watched her for a moment and realized that I had only two hours left to catch the noon plane. I rolled over, rubbed my face for a moment, and asked, "Going out, redhead?"

She was wearing a skirt and blouse that fit a bit too tight, and provided a tantalizing view of the fact that she was a well-stacked woman. She smiled at me coldly, as if she had just met her trick. "You remember that nice little man—the one at the hotel?" she asked. "He has a day off."

"Sure," I said. "About that—"

"He's taking me shopping." She smiled. "I should start paying you back your loan, don't you think?"

"You know what I said before—I don't own you. Scrub floors or whore; you do as you please."

"Or did you want me for something today?"

I got out of bed and began to dress before I answered. "Don't worry about me. I just wanted to tell you that I'd be gone for a few days."

She paused, studying me. "You're finished with what you were doing?" she asked.

"I'm finished enough to make a trip," I said. "I'll be back for a while after that though."

Connie was thoughtful for a moment. "What happens then?"

"What's supposed to happen?" I wanted to know. "Don't sweat it, redhead. The rent's paid here for a couple of months, and you—"

"I can make it on the street," she broke in. "You proved that to me."

I shrugged. "Look. I'll be back in a few days and we can talk about it then," I said. "There's a few things to clear up yet."

"Then you're not really finished."

"I found out what I was paid to find. I'm finished," I said bluntly.

She shook her head. "No," she sighed. "You'll never really be finished." She walked across the room and stood staring at the city from the window. "You'll be back in a few days, and even you don't know where you'll be next. Am I supposed to be here when you get back?"

I stopped buttoning my shirt and glanced at her. "Why not? The apartment's paid for."

Connie said nothing for a long time. Then she sighed, saying, "I wondered how it would end for us." She held up a hand when I started to speak. "No, Jericho, I won't be here when you get back. The one you left me with at the hotel the other night would like to rent an apartment for me. He has a wife and kids, but he's honest enough to admit it."

"You can do better than that," I said.

She smiled. "I'll keep looking while I work."

"So why not stay here then?" I asked, absently. "One apartment is as good as the next." I shrugged. "What's the difference?"

"You are, Jericho. Because I think I'd stay, and I'd wait when you weren't in town, and there's nothing there. That's just the way it would be, until they bury you." She smiled weakly. "The chances for a whore are bad enough without making them impossible."

I avoided her eyes and was silent. Then I said, "No one told you to dream, redhead."

"I don't want to start liking having you around," she said. "So I won't be here when you come back." She smoothed her skirt. "Do you want me to stay until you leave for the airport? I can always see him tomorrow."

I pulled my suitcase from the closet and tossed it on the bed. "Don't worry about me. I can get my ashes hauled in Chicago if I need it. You'd better get going and take care of sugar daddy; he needs the ass worse than I do. And if you're going to make your living on your back, you'll need more than one customer."

I kept my eyes on the suitcase until I heard the door slam.

I listened to the sound of her high heels clicking down the hall, then I snapped the suitcase shut and headed for the airport.

It was Wednesday when I reached Chicago, and I drifted down to Maxwell Street, where I rented a room. Tony Candoli had waited for word on his son for three months now. I thought he could wait a little longer. When no one is expecting you, there is no rush to do unpleasant things. The waiting would also help the heat build in the rat's nest back in Kansas City.

I waited.

I spent my time drinking in the dives near my hotel, where the whiskey mask was stamped on the faces of men who had spent their lives waiting. It was a badge of anonymity. I drank and walked the streets aimlessly, while I thought it out again, checking the details in my mind until each doubt vanished, and I could tell myself that the contract was complete and I was tired. It was the first of August when I woke up tired in my room, and I knew that the drunk was over.

August was the time for dying. The summer dies, and guys like me think of Miami or Los Angeles, or of contracts in any warmer place, and more dying. It made me feel a sense of eagerness to finish it now.

It had been fifteen days since Tony Candoli had fed me whiskey, and sat with his gray sickness, and his fear, while he hoped that I would be the one to make magic. That's me—Judas; I just wave my magic .38 and produce John Candoli to come home and keep the family name alive.

Now he fed me whiskey and laid five thousand dollars on the table beside my chair while he said, "You're back. So you must be finished."

"It's finished as far as it ever will be," I told him, mouthing the first lie I knew I had to tell.

"What did you find out?"

"Not much."

He grunted. "Not much isn't worth any ten grand to me."

"How about four more dead men?" I wanted to know. "Are they worth it? Four more bodies for the family, Candoli." I sipped his whiskey and smiled at him. "Bicek's dead too; you can send someone down there to take over again now. You've got a big dirty bone again to pass on the toughest dog you can find."

"My son?" he asked quietly.

"As dead right now as he'll ever be," I said. "Vanatta is backing the takeover down there. The young group, Candoli. Vanatta, Bicek, and even your man Kapsalis."

"Kapsalis?"

"Sure; why do you think your boy made a try for me with that toad sticker the first night I came here? *Your* orders? No. Kapsalis fingered me as a threat to their little plan even then. So Vanatta sent two of his own men down there to bury me." I shrugged. "You need to do some housecleaning around here."

I paused and smiled at him. "All this is a bonus, Candoli. I'll give it to you because I don't like to walk into a contract like that and not know the odds."

"You sure that my son is dead?" he asked.

"You've got my word on that," I said tightly.

Candoli watched me for a long time, and seemed to shrink into the chair. He sat there with his head making little nodding movements. His eyes were empty as he said, "I'll give you the same contract on Vanatta and Kapsalis."

I shook my head. "You've got fifty men under your thumb, all of them eager and waiting to do you a favor. I don't want it. Hell, put Powell on it. If he's as good with a gun as he is with his mouth, he can handle it. I'm out."

"Why?"

"I've got enough money to lay in the sun for a while. I think I'll do that." I took John Candoli's picture from my pocket and put it on the table. "Forget it, Candoli. There isn't even anyone for you to give it to now."

Candoli kept nodding his head in empty silence. He stared with clouded eyes at the picture I'd dropped on the table, while I picked up the five thousand, went to the door, and let myself out. Powell was waiting for me in the hall.

"How is he, Judas?" he asked eagerly.

I winked at him. "Treat him right," I said. "You may get into the rackets yet. Who knows, he may even start treating you like a son."

I was still laughing when I got into the elevator. I used the telephone in the lobby to call Peggy and I told her the same lies. Then I called the airport and found out when the next plane left for Kansas City. And I wondered briefly how it must feel to know you're dying, and not to have someone around to keep the grave pickers off.

I thought about that for a long time, and decided that dying was one thing a man had to do alone.

eleven

Sometimes you hurt too much to sleep, and you lie restless at night, wishing it were a physical ache, or a gnawing that you could beat down with booze, or heroin, or whatever your kick is.

But even the brain-fogging effects of booze will not reach the hurt that crawls through the emptiness a man can build inside himself. The only way to reach that kind of hurt is to remove it from your mind in the only way you can.

It was Sunday evening in Kansas City when I counted

what I had left of Candoli's ten thousand and felt old and alone in the apartment.

Connie had kept her word, leaving only the faint smell of her perfume in the bedroom when she moved out. I told myself to hell with it, a contract had to be finished sometime, and then I began to pack.

It was warm outside, with a cold storm building in the evening, when I tossed my suitcases in the back of the car and left my latest collection of ghosts in the apartment behind me. It was the sort of evening a man usually spends thinking about a relaxed dinner and a willing woman. I spent it thinking about an old contract and the .38 under my arm, and I hoped that the police had calmed down enough not to have a pickup out on me now.

I hoped too that one more person in the city had calmed down enough to feel safe now. It would be finished then, and I could mark the contract closed, as Candoli thought it was now. It was one thing to finish a job as a client expected but it was another to finish it as the Judas wanted.

I checked my watch and headed for Ninth Street and Greek's place.

Greek was only a little surprised to see me. His face had a gray-white look with dark pockets under his eyes as though he had been losing a lot of sleep waiting for me to show up. He looked at the slight bulge under my arm and he knew I was loaded. Then he looked around for help that wasn't there.

"Hi, slob," I said.

"Judas—I—"

"I know all about it, Greek. I know all about Blacky *and* your lying, you son-of-a-bitch."

"They would have killed me, Judas. I couldn't tell you."

I jerked him forward, slamming his stomach against the bar, then backhanded him hard enough to make the double chin shake like jelly and to redden his frightened eyes.

"Is that why you helped them keep track of me? You put the word out on every move I made right from the start. And you told me nothing but lies."

"I tell you, they would have killed me."

"You didn't figure I would, huh, Greek? That must be why you kept fingering me for a death warrant. You lied yourself right into a corner like you did with Blacky."

The derelicts in the place were watching with interest as they enjoyed Greek's fear. I smiled at him and said, "The truth this time, Greek. Any lies and you'll be in the alley like Blacky was."

Greek shivered and nodded. "Okay, Judas. Okay."

"You fingered Blacky, didn't you?"

"I had to, Judas. They came in late that night and saw Blacky watching them. I never really fingered him, 'cause they knew he ain't just one of the winos."

"It was just a mistake his being here, huh? What happened?"

"So they ask who he is and how close to Perille he might be."

"You're lying, Greek."

"All right; Bicek already knows Blacky. They didn't ask me nothing except where he usually goes. I know they didn't like being seen together like that, so I gave them Anna's address. They would have killed him anyway, Judas. I just—"

"You just made it easier for them to kill him," I said. "Like you tried to make it easier for them to get me. You know what I did when I was in Chicago, Greek?"

He stared at me.

"I gave Candoli your name, Greek. He's unhappy as hell. I gave him your name and told him you were a Bicek man. Do you have any idea what's going to happen to you when he sends some boys down to clean up?"

"Judas—"

"So long, Greek," I said, and let his shirt go. "That Chicago information was a present from Blacky. Now you're going to find out how it is to get fingered. When Candoli starts making it unhealthy, and you need to be looking over your shoulder a lot, think about Blacky."

I left him huddled against the bar, looking suddenly small as he realized that there was no place to hide now where they wouldn't find him. But he was dim-witted enough to start running. I thought Blacky would like to know that Greek would be seeing him every time he looked over his shoulder. Like T-Bone would be seeing me, because his own fear would be as bad as anything I could do to him.

Night had settled in on the city as I got back in the car and began to drive again. It was almost over for this time, but *only* for this time, because in the thing I work for the circle of fear and double cross never ends.

I parked the car near the front entrance of the apartment house where Judy Vann lived, and waited in the dark, remembering the girl who really wanted to find the top and had been willing to kill to help herself reach it. She should have known that I'd be back.

I got that creepy, surprised feeling again, like I'd had when she'd shot me. Or maybe she hadn't thought ahead when she tried to protect her investment by putting slugs into me. I took the pint bottle out of the glove compartment and sipped at the brandy while I waited. Knowing who else was waiting helped the time pass. There was no doubt that I wasn't being given credit for knowing where the rat's nest was. So the waiting there would be for the final results in the Chicago war. If Vanatta won, there would be a leader waiting to take over in Kansas City. If Candoli won, they would start all over again. Anyway, it must be nice to feel that you really couldn't lose in the game.

This time they would lose, I thought. It was in the contract.

It was close to midnight when the one I was waiting for came out of the apartment building and turned up the sidewalk toward my car. I smiled to myself as I stepped out of the shadows and said, "Hello, Johnny."

It surprised him so much I had time to shove him across the sidewalk and into the deeper shadows between the buildings. I let him dig for his gun so I'd know where it was, and just before he dragged it out I whipped my own .38 across his mouth and bottled up his yell into a gagging sound by kneeing him in the crotch.

I held him up against the building, saying, "Be nice, Johnny. That was from your dear old dad. You got a lot more coming from Sanitary Blacky and myself."

Johnny Candoli opened his mouth, then decided not to say much around his shattered teeth.

"You got some hurts coming from Lora Franks too, mister. I can play all sorts of games with you because you're dead as far as your father's concerned, and the rest of these people will forget you in a week." I smiled thinly. "It took me a while to figure out who the boss was, but I'm out of practice. I should have snapped to your game when they told me how you'd killed Black Maria when he was willing to back down. You sure couldn't have done that for Lora Franks; I've seen that doll you had at home."

Anyway, it had taken me a while to figure out why a man would grab right now what he'd be given if he waited. I tightened my grip and shook my head, "Rebelling against the old system. I'm glad I don't belong to the new crowd. But when I figured out what there was in Black Maria's killing; the rest was easy. Black Maria was the only good gunman Mike had; the girl was an excuse. It was a very cool and open operation, Johnny; all you had to do was get rid of Lora later. You did that by giving her a habit and then fixing her face so she wouldn't *want* to come out of any dark corners for the rest of her life."

His shirt and jacket were turning deep red from his bleeding mouth, and he kept dabbing at it like he didn't believe it.

"I'll admit that you Bicek, and Vanatta had a nice takeover going; you would have gotten Kansas City and then Chicago. And there was always Vanatta or your man Kapsalis around to keep your father busy while you and Bicek ran Iron Mike into the ground. It just wasn't like Mike to figure you as being behind a takeover."

I paused a moment. "You were playing it cute, Johnny. You might have gotten away with the biggest piece of the rackets ever to go from syndicate to free lance. Your one fault was your kink, a certain pattern, Johnny; I should have noticed it sooner. You always liked to make the one you shot suffer a lot, didn't you? A man like Bicek would have handled it like business. You shouldn't have liked gut-shooting so much or I wouldn't have realized that even Blacky Shaw wasn't killed in a mugging, but for the same reason Maria had been. You were going to build your own private empire, huh?"

Candoli kept shaking his head and whimpering softly while he pressed his hands to his mouth. Like most of them, he liked to dish out pain but couldn't take it.

I smiled at him. "You had them all scared, Johnny. Greek, T-Bone, Decker, they all knew about your little gut-shooting habit and wouldn't talk. Only Lora Franks knew too, and she didn't have anything left to live for, so she talked. After that, all I needed was a program to read where you stacked in with Vanatta and Kapsalis.

"I should have seen that too, when I realized that Otto and Jo-Jo were Vanatta's men—and they were waiting for me as soon as I got in from Chicago. I suppose Kapsalis had them sent down the first day I was out." I watched him before saying softly, "Either way, Candoli, I knew something stank in that contract to find you—I just didn't know how bad the smell was until I got close to you."

I was silent then, because I didn't care much if he

heard any more about the mistakes he'd made. I'd only wanted him to know that killing Blacky and Maria was part of his mistakes, just as what he'd done to Lora was a mistake.

I hoped that he would remember them all very clearly, because little slips like that could get you killed, and I hoped that he could see them all standing in the shadows with me when I said, "Johnny." He caught the change in my voice. Or maybe he just saw the silencer on the end of my .38 shift slightly as I pulled the hammer back. He pulled his hands down from his face and stared.

And while he was looking, I let him watch the flame dance out from the pistol and lick his jacket just above the belt buckle while the slugs pushed him back.

I had everything I needed in the car—canvas to wrap him with, some wire, and the cement blocks to keep him on the bottom of the river. At least it would keep him there until it wouldn't matter if he drifted loose or not —because no one would be able to guess how long he'd been there by then.

And when it was over, I sighed and looked at the city from the bridge and knew it was finished now. I could feel the dampness of a storm coming in the air and the coldness on the bridge made me shiver. I got back into the car thinking about Connie, and her dreams, and wondered if she had ever spent the winter on the West Coast. Then I shrugged the thought off, and headed the car toward the airport.

Things like Connie were never in the contract.

Format by Yvette A. Vogel
Set in Video Primer
Composed, printed and bound by The Haddon Craftsmen, Inc.
HARPER & ROW, PUBLISHERS, INC.